# NEWSPAPER DAYS

# NEWSPAPER DAYS

*Randy Turner*

iUniverse, Inc.
New York   Bloomington

# Newspaper Days

iUniverse books may be ordered through
booksellers or by contacting:

iUniverse
1663 Liberty Drive
Bloomington, IN 47403
www.iuniverse.com
1-800-Authors (1-800-288-4677)

ISBN: 978-1-4401-8059-0 (sc)
ISBN: 978-1-4401-8060-6 (ebook)

Printed in the United States of America

iUniverse rev. date: 10/06/09

# *DEDICATION*

This is book is dedicated to my parents, Bill and JoAnn Turner, who have encouraged me and put up with me for 53 years, and to all of the reporters, editors, and co-workers who made my 22 years in journalism so memorable.

# *Contents*

# GOODBYE, CARTHAGE PRESS

If you are going to fire someone, do it on a Monday.

That is what the so-called experts say. If you fire someone on Monday, the job search can begin immediately. As managing editor of *The Carthage Press* during the 1990s, I fired a few reporters. It was never easy, but whenever possible, I broke the news to the poor souls on Monday.

On Monday, May 17, 1999, it was my turn.

I had been at work for about an hour when the phone on my desk rang and the publisher, Ralph Bush, asked if I could come into the office for a moment.

This was it. I had known for more than two months that my days at *The Carthage Press* were numbered. After nearly nine years of having uniformly excellent evaluations, I had suddenly received my first bad one two weeks earlier.

I had changed nothing in the way I conducted my job, but all of a sudden everything I did was wrong. I knew enough to figure out that the groundwork for my departure was being carefully laid.

I tested the business manager, Becky VanGilder, by asking her if she could provide the paperwork to sign me up for Liberty Group Publishing's 401K program. Apparently, Becky knew I was not long for *The Press*. She dodged the request and a couple of follow-up requests I made during the next couple of weeks.

During the days that followed that first poor evaluation, I waited until after the office closed and quietly removed my personal items. When the axe finally fell, I did not intend to stay one second longer than necessary.

Expecting to get fired and actually being fired, however, are two different things. Even when you know it is coming, it is a massive blow to the ego. And in the back of my mind, I was still hoping that I was wrong.

The newsroom was only a few feet from the publisher's office. I walked the narrow hallway, passed the receptionist and knocked on Ralph's door.

He motioned for me to come in and pointed toward a chair.

I had the first four words pegged. "Randy, this isn't easy." My heart started pounding- this was it. After steering *The Carthage Press* to more than 100 state, regional, and national awards in less than a decade, I was being cut loose.

Ralph confirmed it moments later. "You have the option of resigning or being fired," he said, his voice remaining calm and carefully modulated.

"I won't resign," I said, trying to stay as calm, though my heart was racing.

"I'm sorry it has to end this way."

"Why am I being fired?"

"We have decided to go in a different direction." Do all bosses take their cues from the same manual?

I asked him to explain. I did not intend to make it easy for him. "We are going to have more of an emphasis on lighter feature stories in the future." he said. My reputation had been made on investigative reporting and an emphasis on hard news, but my staff and I had always been adept at features.

"Do you mean features like the one I did on the Lockwood wedding or my Senior Spotlight profiles on the top 10 seniors at Carthage High School?"

Ralph was squirming and if I still hadn't been feeling the knife in my back, I would have enjoyed it a lot more.

I kept on asking him questions for another 15 or 20 minutes, until I was getting tired of the game and just wanted to get out of there. "I will be out of the building in a few minutes," I said.

"That will be fine, thank you," he said, and I asked the question I wanted to put it off until the very end.

"Does this have anything to do with the libel suit? "

For a moment, I thought he was going to say it did not and that is probably what he should have said. "That played a part in it," he said, quickly adding, "But it was a lot more than just the lawsuit." Those were the last words he said to me.

The walk back down the hallway to the newsroom may have been the longest I have ever taken. I said my goodbyes quickly to staff, grabbed a box and packed the last few items, and left *The Carthage Press* for the final time.

And though I did not know it at the time, I was also walking away from a 22-year career as a reporter and editor and heading for a new career, far removed from journalism.

All of this, thanks to a $1.5 billion libel suit.

# A LITTLE BACKGROUND

Every so often during a school year, something will happen in the news that captures the students' attention, which is saying a lot since most students take pains to stay as far as possible away from anything smacking of news.

One such time was Election Day, November 2000. Before that day, my students at Diamond Middle School in Diamond, Missouri, did not have the slightest interest in whether George W. Bush or Al Gore would be our next president. If I even mentioned the election, their eyes would glaze over as if their parents were lecturing them for the umpteenth time about cleaning their rooms.

That all changed when election night ended and the winner had not been decided. When I arrived at school, I had one student after another yawning and telling me they had stayed up until 3 or 4 a.m. waiting to find out who the winner was. Some of them had wanted to go to bed, but their parents did not want them to miss out on history in the making.

One thing I never told the students- I really wanted Al Gore to win. It had nothing to do with political beliefs since I am an independent who has voted for politicians from both sides and even third party candidates (I was the only person in the small Missouri town of Newtonia to vote for John Anderson over Ronald Reagan and Jimmy Carter in 1980). It had nothing to do with the two candidates' stance on the issues. I was not impressed with George W. Bush or Al Gore (or Ralph Nader, for that matter).

It's just that every time a Bush is in charge, it has been bad news for me.

Ralph Bush fired me from my last newspaper job in 1999 with *The Carthage Press*. His uncle, Richard Bush, fired me from my first newspaper job, in 1978 with the *Newton County News*, and he fired me from my fourth newspaper job, in 1982, again with the *Newton County News*. At least Ralph Bush fired me face to face. Both times his uncle gave me the old heave ho, the message was delivered via the U. S. Mail.

Another Bush was the last thing I needed.

◆          ◆          ◆

My 22-year newspaper career began with a fluke. It was May 1977 and I was in the process of completing my third year of college, working toward an education degree at Missouri Southern State College (now university). I needed a job, and though I had no experience, I applied for the editor's job at the *Newton County News* in Granby, Missouri. My newspaper experience was limited to East Newton High School, where I worked on the school newspaper, the *Fife and Drum*, two poems I submitted to *The Sentry* at Crowder College in Neosho, Missouri; and an angry letter to the editor I wrote to Missouri Southern's newspaper, *The Chart*.

Under normal circumstances I would not have had a prayer of getting the job, but only two people applied for the job, so both of us were hired.

I was 21; my co-editor, Karen Sapp, was 18, and was a few days from graduating from East Newton when she was hired. Coincidentally, I had even dated Karen for a brief time.

Both of us were hired after short interviews with Publisher Richard Bush at his office in the *Neosho Daily News* building. In addition to his duties with the *Newton County News*, he served as the editor of the *Daily*.

After 32 years, I do not remember anything remarkable about that interview except that I got the job. I was driving my parents' car that day and on the way home from the *Daily*,

I took a different route than the one I normally took when driving through Neosho.

Being unfamiliar with the area, I never even saw the stop sign I ran, though I saw, too late, the car that plowed into the right side of the car I was driving.

The accident definitely put a damper on my excitement at being gainfully employed. Surprisingly, after the Neosho Police investigated the accident, even though I was the one who ran the stop sign, I did not get a ticket. A tree had blocked my view of the stop sign. The other driver was ticketed for going too fast. Had I been smart, I would have realized that accident was a sign of things to come.

My job began the next week. The co-editor arrangement worked well for a couple of months, then Karen left to attend college and I was on my own…and did not have the slightest idea of what I was doing.

It would be nice to say that I began my journalism career as a fearless muckraker, ferreting out official corruption and fighting for the little guy. It would be nice, but it would be about as far from the truth as you could get.

I was terrible.

Anyone looking back over the issues of the *Newton County News* that were published between May 1977 and February 1978 will not find more than two or three decent stories I wrote during the entire time, perhaps not that many, and that was not my only failure.

In addition to my reporting and editing duties, I was also the advertising salesman, and I sold little advertising.

I often tell people that during my first time at the *Newton County News* I was the youngest newspaper editor in the state of Missouri…and I was the worst.

My memories of that first stint at the newspaper are few. Thirty-two years have passed and I did not accomplish anything. Karen Sapp and I replaced a woman named Cheryl McFall as editor. Cheryl had only one day to show us the ropes and that was nowhere near enough for me. I spent the next nine months in a daze. I did not have the slightest idea of what I was doing.

So when big news did hit on September 6, 1977, I had no idea of what to do and no one to ask.

◆    ◆    ◆

The blue ink on the flimsy piece of lined notebook paper has faded a little over the past 32 years. I keep it in a gray, metal box with some of my other valuables like important letters, contracts, insurance policies, and all of the other supposedly important things that these heavy-duty containers are designed to protect.

Debbie Kruse handed me that sheet and another one day while she was a sophomore and I was a junior at East Newton High School. I was on the school newspaper, *The Fife and Drum* (that name is a perfect example of the danger of having Patriots as a school nickname), and Debbie wanted the poems on those two pages to be printed. The author did not know Debbie was going to do that. Both poems were done in free verse and they were quite good. I agreed to put them in the newspaper and after discussing it with the editor, Paul Richardson, the poems were added to the list of things that would go into the next edition.

"Remember the days, when we were young and free to roam and play like goofy kids." Those were the first few words of Barbara McNeely's poem, "Remember the Days." When her poems were published, she acted like she was upset, but I could see she was secretly pleased about the universal positive reaction she received.

Her words became more poignant on September 6, 1977, when Barbara, then a sophomore at Missouri Southern State College, was stabbed to death in the parking lot at Northpark Mall in Joplin. My mother broke the news to me about

Barbara's death and I was numb for quite a while after that. Though I was the editor of the weekly newspaper for the community where Barbara was born and raised, I did not write a single word about her murder or the subsequent arrest and trial of the killer.

Eulah Hawkins, whose work for the newspaper was normally limited to a weekly column, covered Barbara's murder and the subsequent trial of her killer for the *Newton County News*. Eulah was a friend of the McNeely family and her emotions were always present in the coverage. It was raw and it was well done…but I never contributed a thing, something I regret to this day.

I don't know if it was fear or general incompetence, or a combination of both, but I missed an opportunity to deal with her death and to help others deal with it. As years passed, I have tried to tell myself that I was too young, which is probably true, but I still feel the guilt over abdicating my responsibility and handing it over to Eulah Hawkins. Especially since Barbara and I had been good friends since high school.

I vividly remember standing in the Granby United Methodist Church during Barbara's funeral. Not once did it occur to me that coverage of that event could have helped a grieving community. It did occur to me later. Ironically, during my time at *The Carthage Press* I was always the one who covered the funerals of those who died long before their time.

But I did not do that for one who meant more to me than any of them.

I can't imagine how the McNeely family dealt with that tragedy, Her parents, her brother, her baby sister who never had a chance to get to know Barbara. Barbara had done some work for me, typing manuscripts for me in high school as I tried unsuccessfully to become a published teenaged novelist.

For years, I thought about Barbara every day. I could hear her voice clear as a bell in my mind.

One of the saddest days in my life came a few years ago when it occurred to me that I couldn't remember what her voice sounded like. Every once in a while, it will come to me, but it makes me sad that I can't conjure up that voice when I recollect conversations we had and things she said. All I remember are the words.

A lunatic who mistook her for the mother he hated silenced her voice after she had barely spent two decades on this earth. Barbara, who worked at the J. C. Penney store at Northpark Mall, had just returned from a trip to another store, when William McMurray leaped out of the shadows, and stabbed her dozens of times. McMurray, a student at Ozark Bible College, was found not guilty of her murder after a successful use of the insanity defense. I will never forget how the good people from Ozark Bible College and Rev. Cecil Todd of Revival Fires, were far more concerned with the killer than they were with the family of his victim.

Barbara's murderer has been a free man for several years, thanks to the Missouri Department of Health and former Attorney General Bill Webster, who defended the department's decision to release the killer back into society. Last I heard, and this was several years ago, Barbara's killer was married, had children, and was working as an EMT. He was leading the kind of life Barbara should have had, but never had the chance.

Three decades have passed, but it is the story I did not cover that haunts my memory and I can hardly remember anything that I did write during that time.

◆     ◆     ◆

Not all of my memories of my short time at the Newton County News are bad ones. For a few months during that time, I had a diversion that almost made my laughable introduction to journalism worthwhile. It happened in a tiny store a few doors down from the Newton County News office.

The name of the place was the Ice Cream Boll, and East Newton High School band instructor Don Boll and his wife Mary, owned it.

I have always loved ice cream but until the summer of 1977, it was never an obsession with me. And to be honest, it really wasn't the ice cream; it was one of the young ladies who worked there. I made it a point to stop by the Ice Cream Boll and buy something. If this girl was not working, I just said a quick hello and was on my way.

For a long time, I did not say much to the girl, other than hello and how are you and maybe a comment or two about the weather. Before long, on days when business was slow, she started talking to me. On one memorable day, I stayed a bit longer than usual and the business manager at the *Newton County News* office, Linda Siler, called the Ice Cream Boll because someone had arrived early for an interview. I had to step behind the counter to take the call and after the conversation was over, I put the receiver on the hook and saw this young woman who had become almost the center of my existence standing between the gate that led to the dining area and me. I almost said, "Excuse me," but suddenly I had a different idea. I lightly touched her shoulder, she turned around, and seconds later, we were kissing.

It was not the first time I had kissed a girl (and I had enjoyed the previous experiences), but this was the first time I truly understood why the poets and the movies romanticized the act.

After the kiss, I waited for the slap that was sure to come, or for her to scream for the police (and the police station was located directly behind the Ice Cream Boll). After an awkward second that seemed more like an hour, she smiled and said, "It took you long enough!" It may have taken weeks to set up our first kiss, but its successor came seconds later.

Unfortunately (for me, at least), it was a short-lived romance. A few months later, she and her family moved to Alaska. For a few months, we stayed in contact (and I ran up a sizable phone bill) but she was realistic enough to know it was time for us to head our separate ways.

More than 32 years have passed, but I can still remember everything about that summer day when we shared out first kiss. I remember how she was dressed, how her lips tasted, and the sound of her voice as she spoke those words that were far better than any I had anticipated.

That summer romance, which extended into the early autumn, helped me survive and helped me deal with the aftermath of the death of Barbara McNeely. After the young woman and her family left for Alaska, the rest of my time at the newspaper was sheer torture.

Finally, in February 1978, Richard Bush put me (and the *Newton County News* readers) out of my misery nine months into the job, sending me a letter telling me my services were no longer needed.

It was my first professional failure. A few people who have watched my career over the past three decades would say I should have taken that as a sign from God that journalism was not the field for me. Instead, I took my firing as a challenge. Though I was still attending classes at Missouri Southern, intending to be a teacher, I did not want to leave the newspaper business as a failure.

◆　　　◆　　　◆

With a couple months left in my fourth year of college, still shy of enough credits to earn my degree, I had a burning desire to prove that I could succeed as a reporter.

One morning I spotted an advertisement placed by the *Lamar Democrat* in the *Joplin Globe*. The *Democrat* was looking for a general assignment reporter. The only problem was the job needed to be filled immediately and I still had two months left at MSSC and I was not going to throw away my tuition money.

Nevertheless, I mailed in a resume and the two or three good clips I had, and even though I specified in my cover letter that I could not take the job, I still wanted the *Democrat* to know that I was interested in someday working there.

For some reason, despite my not being available until summer, *Democrat* Editor Lou Nell Clark called me in for an interview. The job went to a reporter named Steve Painter, but I must have made a favorable impression. When May rolled around, Lou Nell called and said the *Democrat* had an opening for a sports editor and asked if I would be interested. I jumped at the opportunity.

So in May 1978, I became sports editor of the *Lamar Daily Democrat*, pulling down $130 a week. At the *Newton County News*, I had no one available to ask how to do things. Richard Bush was an absentee publisher who only stopped by two times that I can recall during the nine months I was there. At the *Democrat*, I had people ready and willing to help me. Russell Pierson, the composing room foreman for more than 20 years, helped me with layout, while Dorothy Parks, a typesetter who was far more than a typesetter, helped me with background on the people and places of Lamar and Barton County, and she was also a stickler for spelling and grammar.

More than anyone I learned from Lou Nell Clark. Though Lou Nell had her detractors in Lamar, I appreciated her approach to journalism and I patterned mine after it. She fought for the little guy and to Lou Nell, the most criminal thing a reporter could do was to be boring.

Though my main job was sports, I also served as a general assignment reporter. For the eight months the job lasted, it was heaven.

Unfortunately, the *Lamar Democrat* was the first place for me to learn about the evils of chain ownership. The week I arrived at the *Democrat* was the week Boone Newspapers took over the company from a man named David Palmer.

It did not take long for the cuts to begin and the newsroom was no exception. I didn't know this at the time, but I found out later that I nearly lost my job in the late summer of '78. Lou Nell had been told to get rid of me because one person had to be cut from the newsroom and I was the last one hired. She refused and eventually got her way. Steve Painter was placed in charge of the weekly paper Boone Newspapers owned 25 miles from Lamar, the *Lockwood Luminary-Golden City Herald*. My job was saved for the time being. When November arrived, Boone Newspapers decided to bring in a man named Don Davis to succeed Lou Nell as managing editor, with Lou Nell staying as a reporter. It was a disaster.

Don Davis was not a people person, and that was something you have to be in order to be a successful small-town newspaper editor. He was in his late 20s, but his blond hair was already nearly gone and from his considerable heft, it appeared that Don Davis and exercise were not on speaking terms.

A few years later when I returned to the *Democrat*, Publisher Doug Davis (no relation to Don) and I found papers from 1978 that indicated Boone Newspapers executives were aware of all kinds of problems with Don Davis' personality and, instead of getting rid of him, decided to inflict him on Lamar.

In December, the newspaper was once again ordered to cut one person from the news staff. This time, there was no doubt about it. It was my head on the chopping block.

Publisher Dennis Garrison called me into his office and gave me the bad news, but he said there was a job open for me in the company- as editor of the *Lockwood Luminary-Golden City Herald*. If I took the job, he said, Steve Painter would be history.

Since I knew Painter was making $170 a week, $40 a week more than I was, I said, "I could use $170 a week."

"Well, you would still be making $130 a week."

I said thanks but no thanks.

I said my goodbyes to the people on my sports beat, including Lamar High School Football Coach Chuck Blaney, who gave me some valuable advice. "Randy, you wanted to be a teacher. You should go back and get your degree. You would be a great teacher." I remembered that advice and eventually, I followed it. But I had another stop before my return to Missouri Southern State College.

◆     ◆     ◆

I had barely started receiving unemployment checks when I received an unexpected offer to step right back into journalism.

It was early January 1979 when *Lamar Democrat* Publisher Dennis Garrison called me at home in Newtonia and once again offered me the position of editor of the *Lockwood Luminary-Golden City Herald*. Apparently, Steve Painter had left suddenly to take a reporting position with the *Springfield News-Leader*, and judging from the long distance phone bill he left behind, he had been desperate to get away from Lockwood.

"We can pay you $170 a week now," Dennis said.

I don't know what got into me, but I responded, "That would have been good enough last month, but it isn't now."

After about five minutes of haggling, I agreed to take the *Luminary-Herald* job at a salary of $180 a week. The newspaper operated out of Lockwood and I immediately fell in love with the town of 900 residents.

For the first month, Boone Newspapers paid for me to stay at the Star Motel. After that, I was able to find a rental house for $100 a month two doors down from the high school.

What wasn't there to like about Lockwood? The people were friendly, the town had two fast food places, John's and C&J that had great burgers, foot-long hot dogs, and soft drinks (and gorgeous waitresses), and I developed a style that worked for me during the next decade as I worked in weekly and twice-weekly newspapers- I gathered as much news as I could until deadline day, then I began a marathon writing session. It probably was not good for my health since I was staying up until 3 or 4 in the morning on deadline day, then getting back up at 6 to take the paper into Lamar to be printed.

Two months into the job, my boss, Dennis Garrison, was fired. And Boone Newspapers put a man named Tommy Wilson in his place. Wilson was a tall, smarmy guy with a dark mustache who clearly thought he was God's gift to women and I could tell quickly that whatever bad thoughts I had about him were nothing compared to how he felt about me.

Still, he was in Lamar and I was in Lockwood, so I did not worry much about it. I just kept doing my job and collecting my $180 a week. I even picked up a few extra bucks umpiring Little League games.

The summer months in Lockwood were great. In addition to the newspaper work and umpiring, I was playing semi-pro baseball for the Aroma Express (a Granby team named after a small ghost town a few miles from Granby) on weekends, and writing a murder mystery on the Underwood portable typewriter at the *Luminary-Herald*.

I was ready to give that all up, when I heard that Tommy Wilson had fired Don Davis as the *Lamar Democrat* editor. By this time, I had long since overcome the feelings of failure I had when I was fired by Richard Bush at the *Newton County News*. And even though it would mean being in close proximity to Tommy Wilson, I wanted the chance to be the new editor.

On a Wednesday morning when we were in Lamar to get the *Luminary-Herald* printed, I got up the nerve to go for the job. "Tommy, I would like to apply for the editor's position," I said.

He laughed. "Randy, just keep doing your job at Lockwood. You are too young to be an editor. We need someone with a lot more experience." At the time I was 23 years old. I could see the wisdom of what he said, though I knew full well I could handle the responsibility.

And, of course, Tommy hired a 22-year-old he knew from Arkansas, David Farnham, as his new editor.

I could see the handwriting on the wall.

Meanwhile, Boone Newspapers continued to cut jobs at the *Lamar Democrat* and soon the cuts reached Lockwood. In early October, Tommy Wilson breezed into the *Luminary-Herald* office on the day we were putting together that week's paper and said, "I wanted to tell y'all, this is the last newspaper we are going to be publishing. We're shutting down the *Luminary-Herald*." He turned to our advertising saleswoman, Donna Shaw, and said, "Donna, we're going to take you to Lamar with us." He turned back toward me and there was a crooked smile on his face. "Randy, we're not going to be taking you." He seemed to relish that statement.

And that was the entire announcement. He was in the building for less than five minutes and then left us to put together the final edition.

In hindsight, Tommy probably wishes he had waited until after the newspaper was put to bed to make the announcement. By telling us late in the afternoon, he gave me time to write a farewell column, and I took full advantage of the opportunity to rip chain ownership of newspapers.

No one caught the column and *Luminary-Herald* readers received it in the mail that Thursday.

Tommy Wilson was livid, but before he had a chance to do anything about it, I hit him with a bill for $700 worth of mileage and told him I had consulted with a lawyer. I actually had not talked to a lawyer at that point, but the day I sent

Tommy the letter, I stopped by the law offices of Edison Kaderly on the Lamar Square.

Kaderly, who was no fan of Tommy Wilson, would not accept any money from me. He told me he did not think I needed a lawyer. "If you don't get your money in the next few days, give me a call."

Edison had read the situation correctly. In a couple of days, I received a letter from Tommy Wilson, ripping me up one side and down the other for my farewell column and my lack of professionalism. He said I had burned my bridges behind me and would never work in newspapers again.

I did not care. I was going to take Chuck Blaney's advice-return to Missouri Southern State College and get my teaching degree. As far as I was concerned, newspapers were a part of my history. It was time for me to grow up.

# *RETURNING TO THE NEWTON COUNTY NEWS*

I had one year left to get my teaching degree, so I returned to Missouri Southern in the fall of 1980. By this time, I was living with my parents in Newtonia and making money by telemarketing for Editor Emery Styron at my first newspaper, the *Newton County News*. I did well. I generally could sell about five subscriptions in an hour and I received a generous cut for each subscriber after the newspaper had the money in its hands.

After starting with that job, Emery began using me for some sports and news coverage and, as I returned to MSSC in the fall, Emery announced he was leaving the newspaper, and once again Richard Bush put me in charge of news and advertising.

The good news was I was much better at news than I was during my first stint at the newspaper. The bad news- I still could not sell advertising.

During that time, two of my Aroma Express baseball teammates, Steve Ray and Mark Judd, and I rented the apartment above the *Newton County News* office in downtown Granby, with each of us paying $35 a month.

I planned to actually live there. The other two planned to use it for their romantic trysts with young area females. Fortunately, for me at least, they didn't have that many romantic trysts, so most nights I was able to stay in the apartment and just walk downstairs to work the next morning.

One evening, however, I returned to the *Newton County News* office to finish a couple of stories, with plans of climbing upstairs to the apartment and taking a nap.

As I started working on the first story, I heard music coming from the eight-track player in the bedroom, which was right above my office.

Soon the music was accompanied by sounds of another kind. One of my roommates had finally managed to get lucky. To this day, I have a hard time listening to anything by the Lettermen.

It was a long night.

During the spring of 1981, I began my student teaching at Diamond Junior High School, teaching eighth grade history and ninth grade government. It was a killer schedule. I got up every morning at 6, arrived at school at 7:30, left at 3:30, worked at the *Newton County News* until 11 p.m., and then did lesson plans and grade papers until 2 a.m., getting up four hours later to start the cycle again.

Thankfully, I was much younger then and could handle that kind of schedule. Still, when my student teaching was over, I was a certified teacher and ready to leave newspapers for good.

As I searched for a teaching job, it did not take me long to discover that there was no market for high school/junior high school social studies teachers who did not coach. I had coached summer teams in baseball and fast pitch girls and women's softball for years, but there was no way I had the knowledge to coach basketball or football. Write about them, absolutely. Coach them, no chance.

When I saw job openings, I submitted my resume, but I failed to land any interviews, until a history job opened at a small high school in the far southwest corner of Missouri near the Arkansas line.

I was prepared to answer any questions the principal had about how I would teach history or geography or government. I shouldn't have spent the time preparing. My conversation with the principal lasted more than an hour and a half. During that time, not one question was asked about classroom teaching. It was clear that teaching history was a secondary concern as far as this job, and this principal, was concerned.

I answered one question after another about how I would coach basketball. A lot of the questions were about girls basketball and how I would coach it and how I would deal with the players. After all, the principal revealed to me in a conspiratorial whisper, "Girls are different than boys." I regretted I had not brought my notepad to jot down that pearl of wisdom.

Whoever was hired, the principal said, would coach both the boys and girls basketball teams, as well as the baseball and softball teams. "We'll pay the person we hire extra for that," the principal said. "Don't worry."

When the interview concluded, I left the school firmly convinced that I was going to be offered the job, but I did not feel good about it.

When I returned to Granby, I called some old friends from that area to ask about the school and the job and learned quickly this was not where I wanted to have my first teaching job. Two years earlier, the man who was coaching the girls basketball team had an affair with one of his players and, in fact, had run off with her.

To keep that from happening again, the board of education decided to hire a woman. Apparently, the board did not do enough research on the sexual orientation of the new coach who also had an affair with one of her players.

Since they couldn't drop the girls basketball program altogether, thanks to Title IX, when the boys basketball coach resigned to take a higher-paying job, the board decided to hire someone to coach both teams. This way, the theory went, the coach would not have enough time to have an affair with one of his players.

I called the principal the next day and told him I did not want to be considered for the job. That was the only interview for a teaching job I had. Fortunately, I still had my job at the *Newton County News*.

And for the next few months, I had a great time. For the first time, I was able to devote a considerable amount of time to coverage of city council and school board meetings and found I enjoyed them, even when they lasted until all hours of the morning.

A friend of mine named Scott White, who was a cartoonist, began doing a weekly drawing for the paper called "White's Spot," a takeoff on the name of Granby's most popular tavern, The White Spot, the favorite hangout of Police Chief Duane Beaver, who sometimes played dominoes at the bar for hours.

Scott, a mutual friend of ours named Danny Tanner, and I came up with ideas for the cartoons, many of which came from Granby's political battles.

During my second stint at the *Newton County News*, Granby had a newly-elected mayor, liquor store owner Bob Snyder, a short bald man with a mustache, who was as friendly a person as you would ever want to meet, but who had no business being the mayor.

One of my first big stories was when Snyder was convinced that one of the city council members, Helen Lee, was trying to make sure a company connected to her husband would get the city's cable television contract. Snyder pushed for impeachment proceedings against Mrs. Lee and when the hearings were held, she held onto her job by one vote.

That angered Snyder, who said if the city council was not going to back him, he would quit- and he did. Then before the next council meeting when his resignation would have been the first item on the agenda, Snyder withdrew his resignation. Shortly after the meeting began, Snyder blew up again, and resigned a second time, this time for good. (Or at least until he ran again a few years later, was once again elected, and once again resigned a few months into his term.) Snyder's departure in 1981 enabled the city of Granby to make history. Granby's first woman mayor, Joyce Mann, replaced him but the city could not even get that right.

Granby's first woman mayor was a Mann.

As much fun as Granby's mayors were, they were only the secondary source of entertainment in city government. The real story in Granby was the police department, particularly the city marshal, the aforementioned Duane Beaver. City marshal was an elected position in Granby, so there was nothing the city council could do about the popular Beaver.

When Beaver walked into a room, there was no doubt who was in charge, and it was not just because of the 400 plus pounds he weighed.

Much of the time, he was easygoing, but when he became angry and his face turned a bright crimson, you did not want to be the object of his rage.

Though the city council could do nothing about Beaver, it was in charge of hiring deputies and it never chose anyone that Beaver liked.

Oftentimes, Beaver would pull the police cruiser into the city's most popular restaurant, Reta's, and give anyone who stopped by his table the lowdown on what "those idiots" the city council had hired had done.

The battle for control of the police department was the main story during my second tour with the *Newton County News*, but I also had numerous run-ins with police officers during those months.

One time, Duane Beaver became incensed when we ran a Scott White cartoon which showed him, his two deputies Lester Edgar and Teddy "Sherlock" Brock, both of whom also weighed in the neighborhood of 300 pounds, all in wheelchairs in the year 2011, still complaining about the police department.

It was the first time I could remember Duane setting foot in the newspaper office, and he was none too pleased. "I don't mind the cartoon," he said, though obviously he did. "It looks just like Lester Ray and Teddy, but that doesn't look a thing like me."

He could take the criticism; he just wanted to make sure the depiction was accurate.

Another time, we had to call the police to let them know that a dangerous situation was about to take place at the apartment above the newspaper office.

Romantic problems were taking place for one of my roommates, the one who had used the Greatest Hits of the Lettermen as background music for the first time he and his girlfriend took their relationship to a more physical level.

Unfortunately, her father was none too happy about this relationship and I received a phone call from the girl telling me that her father was headed for Granby with a gun and was going to kill my friend.

If the situation had not seemed so serious at the time, I probably would have enjoyed it more. When Danny Tanner, who was at the apartment when the call came in, decided to go outside, he shouted, "This is Danny Tanner. I am not Steve Ray. I am not Randy Turner. Please don't shoot." Those words did not seem funny at the time.

I called the Granby Police Department when I saw the girl's father pull in at the Fastrip store across from the *Newton County News* office.

"He may have a gun," I told Deputy Lester Ray Edgar.

"Don't worry," he said. "We know how to deal with these situations. We will be as unobtrusive as possible."

A few moments later, as the girl's father was getting gas for his vehicle, two unobtrusive police cars, sirens sounding and lights flashing, pulled into the Fastrip parking lot. Nothing happened, my friend and his girlfriend eventually broke up, and as far as I know, none of us have listened to the Lettermen to this day.

◆         ◆         ◆

The last few weeks of my time at the Newton County News were also filled with controversy. I was dating a teacher from an area school district, who told me that the drug situation was bad in her school.

I was inspired to find out just how bad the situation was in the East Newton School District. So I took an unscientific survey and talked to about two dozen teachers and students. The situation was worse than I had imagined. The consensus was that between 80 and 90 percent of the students had tried alcohol and that it was a serious problem for 30 to 40 percent of the student body. A smaller, but still substantial portion of the student body had tried marijuana. I also discovered that drug sales were taking place on Granby's Main Street, only a few feet away from where I was living.

So the next week, I wrote a story about the survey, and a front page editorial saying it was time for something to be done about the easily accessible drugs in Granby.

For the next several days, the Granby Police harassed the dope dealers and anyone who was coming to Main Street for a buy. In the process of doing that, of course, they harassed anyone else who was on Main Street and was of a certain age.

One night, as I returned from a meeting, four young men approached me in the alley by the *Newton County News* office, two of them carrying baseball bats, and one with a very visible knife.

The leader of the group stepped to within two feet of me and slurred, "Why did you write that stuff about us?" Before I could answer, he said, "Let's teach him a lesson."

Before my lesson began, I said, "Guys, wait a minute. Wait a minute. This is not going to last forever. They are going to hassle you for a few days then things will go back to normal. If they don't, I'll come back here and you can beat me up."

That caught them off guard. It caught me off guard, too. I didn't know I could think that fast and I still was not sure this was going to save me.

Finally, one of them said, "All right, but we'll be back."

On a Friday night a few days later, as I was watching a midnight movie in my apartment, I heard glass shattering downstairs. I ran down to the newspaper office and saw that a large rock had been hurled through the window.

I called the Granby Police Department, which promptly sent someone an hour and a half later. The person who threw the rock was never caught.

Fortunately for me, the Granby Police Department's war on drugs only lasted a few more days and I never met face-to-face with any more unhappy young gentlemen, nor did I have any more rocks thrown through the window.

That was not the only fallout from my articles though. I was banned from covering East Newton activities, though Superintendent Dalton Ham finally relented and East Newton High School did a survey of its own. Reporter Bill Ball publicized that survey in an article in the Neosho Daily News.

The article ripped into my survey calling it fiction and released the results of the survey that had been conducted by the school. After reading the survey, I knew I had missed the biggest story in the Granby area- these kids were angels.

Without even questioning the results, Bill Ball parroted the information that only 10 percent of the students at East Newton High School had ever had a drop of beer.

This wasn't East Newton High School, I thought, this is the Mormon Tabernacle Choir.

And that set the stage for Scott White's farewell cartoon, and it was a great way for him to make his exit, though we did not know that was what it was going to be.

Scott drew a picture of two teenagers with halos over their heads carrying ballots to a ballot box that was labeled "East Newton Drug Poll." The caption read, "First Annual East Newton Naivety Pageant."

Not long after that cartoon, in early January 1982, Richard Bush sent me another letter telling me my services were no longer needed.

The letter started:

*Dear Randy:*

*I was planning on talking to you Tuesday, but since you all switched around, I was unable to do so. If you want to talk further about this, I would be glad to see you next Tuesday or at your convenience.*

In the next paragraph, Richard finally got around to the purpose of the letter:

*As you know, I have let you all know recently that the Newton County News financial picture was extremely bleak. We have been losing money at a pace greater than the company has been able to absorb, or at least we are unwilling to continue doing so.*

*We have not made final plans for the future of the Newton County News, but it is either going to be cut back substantially, merged in with operations in Neosho (the Neosho Daily News owned the newspaper) or cut out completely.*

*That decision may be some weeks away.*

*Meanwhile, Kenneth (Neosho Daily News Publisher Kenneth Cope) and I have decided we must have some staff cutback so I am hereby notifying you that your job will be terminated effective after the working day on Thursday, January 28.*

In the remainder of the letter, he told me not to write about anything controversial during my final two weeks, not to write any columns and not to "air dirty laundry," and not to run any more Scott White cartoons.

Bush concluded:

> *You can be assured that while I have occasionally disagreed with your editorial policy, this has nothing to do with this termination. As before, the basic reasons are that the newspaper has again fallen into losing money and we just cannot continue this way.*
>
> *Thank you for trying.*

The firing did not come as a surprise. I had been halfway expecting it for months, but Richard Bush's manner of doing it was bush league, if you will pardon the pun.

This was the second time he had fired me by the mail. He could not even bring himself to deliver the news face to face. And even worse, he had forced me to wade through five paragraphs of mind-numbing prose before he got around to delivering the message.

After a couple of weeks, I moved out of the apartment above the *Newton County News* office and moved back in with my ever-patient parents who had to be wondering if their son was ever going to be a success at anything.

I was rapidly approaching my 26th birthday, and still had not progressed much past minimum wage, dead-end newspaper jobs. And now I didn't even have one of those.

I worked as a substitute teacher in the Diamond and Pierce City school districts for the remainder of the 1981-82 school year. During part of the summer, I managed the city of Granby's recreation program, preparing the fields for play, umpiring, and taking care of scheduling. During all of that time, I continued looking for a teaching position, but nothing was available.

When the fall of 1982 arrived, I still did not have full-time work, but the Pierce City School District was keeping me working three or four days a week, substituting in high school, junior high school, and worst of all, elementary school. I was always scared to death that one of the kids was going to have a bathroom accident or something of that nature during my watch, but fortunately that never happened.

Since it was too late to get a teaching job for the 1982-1983 school year, I reluctantly began considering journalism jobs. I talked briefly with Jim Wallace, publisher of the *Greenfield Advertiser*, who was ready to put me to work, but decided he could not afford to hire anyone.

I also was considered for a reporting position with the *El Dorado Springs Sun*, but that fell through. I had just returned home from subbing for a fourth grade class at Pierce City Elementary (a nightmare job if ever one existed) when I received a call from Doug Davis, who had replaced Tommy Wilson as publisher of the *Lamar Democrat* in March 1981. "I am looking for a news editor who knows Lamar. Would you be interested?"

Considering the column I wrote when I left Boone Newspapers in October 1979, I was surprised I would be even considered, but I was intelligent enough not to say anything about that.

"Sure."

We set up a time for an interview and within a few days, I had the job that Tommy Wilson had said I was too young for three years earlier. I was the new editor of the *Lamar Democrat*.

# *LAMAR DEMOCRAT REVISITED*

The *Lamar Democrat* I returned to in November 1982 was a far cry from the newspaper I remembered from three years earlier when I was still working for the company at the *Lockwood Luminary-Golden City Herald*.

It took me a while to get filled in on what had happened during the three years I was gone, but there was no doubt the best thing that could have happened to me was losing out to Dave Farnham for the editor position. (Actually, Tommy Wilson never even considered me for it.)

The Wilson-Farnham team was a nightmare for the *Democrat* and for the city of Lamar. Almost immediately after he was hired, Farnham began to take on city government and the establishment in Lamar. Not that there was anything wrong with that. The *Lamar Democrat* had a rich history of going after the truth dating back to the era from 1900 to 1972 when Arthur Aull and his daughter, Madeleine Aull VanHafften, had published the newspaper.

Farnham, with Wilson's blessing, however, was relentlessly negative, to the point of not offering coverage of the many positive things that were going on in the city.

Things got so bad that a group of businessmen, led by Dan Arnold, owner of the Lamar Supermarket, the Democrat's biggest advertiser, convinced a man named Jim Peters from Arnold's home town, Butler, Missouri, to start a shopper, similar to the *XChanger*, one he started in that town which eventually drove the Butler newspaper out of business.

That was not the intent of the Lamar businessmen, who realized the need for a newspaper in a thriving community, but the fortunes of the *Lamar Democrat* sank quickly after Jim Peters started *XChanger 2*.

All of the Lamar Supermarket advertising, which had taken up two to four full pages in the *Democrat* each week, was relocated to the shopper. Other businesses quickly followed and revenues plummeted for the *Democrat*.

Seeing the handwriting on the wall, Wilson and Farnham left the paper in early 1981, not giving their superiors at Boone Newspapers much notice. Even worse, the departure came at the worst time of the year for any newspaper- the deadline for the annual Progress Edition was only a week away, and little advertising had been sold.

In an attempt to salvage the newspaper, Boone sent a company troubleshooter, Alabaman Doug Davis, to take over in February 1981.

Davis pulled the newspaper through the Progress Edition, but quickly realized Wilson and Farnham had damaged the reputation of the *Democrat* so much, that his job was not just to win back advertisers, but to make sure the publication continued to exist.

To save money, Davis dropped the *Democrat's* contract with Associated Press and reduced the number of pages in each edition to eight.

The stroke of genius that quickly put Davis' stamp on the *Lamar Democrat* was a daily page one feature he started called "Today in Barton County." Each day a different member of the community wrote a column. The authors ranged from city officials to members of Lamar's Community Betterment organization to the woman who quickly became the most anticipated Today in Barton County writer, Reba Young.

Mrs. Young, a descendant of Lamar's first lawman, the fabled Wyatt Earp, regaled readers with her memories of growing up at the turn of the century. Her eye for detail and her sharp sense of humor made this woman, who was already in her 80s when she began the column, an immediate hit. Reba, whose husband Charles was Barton County's last surviving World War I veteran, and the other Today in Barton County writers, created a positive buzz around the *Democrat*, something it had not seen since Tommy Wilson and Dave Farnham had led the paper into its dark days.

While Davis' moves saved the newspaper, it was quickly evident it could no longer be published five days a week. Davis made the *Democrat* a weekly, jam-packed with local news. Still, it was hard for the community to get used to the loss of its afternoon daily.

Generations of young Lamar residents had received their first jobs delivering the *Democrat*. Now the newspaper would come to residents through the mail.

That was the situation when I returned to Lamar in November 1982. It was not until years later that I discovered I was not the only one Davis considered for the news editor position. I was selected over Lou Nell Clark, the woman who had been my number one supporter during my first stint at the *Democrat*. The reason for the choice, I was told, was because people thought Lou Nell would be too much of a troublemaker. I don't know if I would have accepted the position if I had known it came at Lou Nell's expense, but I was happy to be back in Lamar.

My job was to beef up the newspaper's news and sports coverage and I wasted no time doing so, I increased coverage of Barton County government, the Lamar school system, area towns, and Lamar and area sports. For the most part, I was a one-man crew, though a woman in her 60s, Judy Probert, a former editor at the *Luminary-Herald*, wrote about Golden City news, and Doug Davis covered the Lamar City Council and the Barton County Memorial Hospital Board of Trustees. The office manager, Opal Sims, wrote a popular cooking column, Sims' Simmerings, which had been suggested by Doug. Each week, she turned the spotlight on a person in the community, writing a feature and printing three or four recipes from that person.

The beefed up newspaper quickly picked up circulation and by August 1983, Doug elected to publish twice a week, Tuesdays and Thursdays.

My time in Lamar was made even more special during those early years thanks to a conversation that never should have taken place in the late spring of 1983.

I had scheduled an interview with a Lamar High School senior, one of a series I did each year on graduating seniors who deserved recognition. I was on time, but the girl was nowhere in sight. Since the meeting was at a fast food restaurant, Spanky's, I sat down, ordered, and waited for the girl to arrive.

One of her friends and classmates, an attractive tall and slender young woman with long brown hair and a captivating smile, was seated at a nearby booth. She saw me, knew about the interview, and told me the girl was going to be late. We began talking and I quickly found myself hoping my interview subject would never arrive.

After that, I began running into the girl here and there and soon we were dating and even talking about marriage. Between this romance and my job, I was thoroughly enjoying my life. For the first and only time during my newspaper years, I was actually abandoning my job on Friday and Saturday nights on a regular basis and going out for dinner, movies, or occasionally just watching videos and eating pizza in my apartment.

The romance came crashing down around me in early 1984, just a few months before we were supposed to be married. I had screwed up the best thing that had happened to me.

As always, I threw myself into my work, putting in 60 to 70 hours on the slow weeks and more when events were piling up.

In March 1985, the *Democrat* sold, and the newspaper was returned to local ownership for the first time since the Aull family sold it to the Kirkpatricks of Warrensburg in 1972. Doug Davis bought the paper, something we announced with 144-point type (72 point is about the biggest normally used in newspapers.) screaming "Democrat sells." Things were looking up for the newspaper.

But despite the turnaround of the *Lamar Democrat*, the *XChanger 2* continued to drain money from us. Lamar Supermarket ran all of its advertising with the shopper and when the supermarket's only competitor, Lamar IGA, went out of business, it cost us another page of advertising each week. The arrival of Lamar's first Wal-Mart store also caused problems. Wal-Mart placed almost no newspaper advertising, preferring direct mail, and its presence caused many of the downtown shops, including some that were faithful *Democrat* advertisers, to go out of business.

Faced with declining revenues, Doug Davis took a dramatic step. He called me into his office and said he was going to double the newsstand price of the paper and also increase the subscription price.

"We're going to lose subscribers," I said.

"No, we won't," he said with a certainty that surprised me. "We are not going to lose readers because we are going to increase our coverage."

In order to accomplish that, Doug gave me the go ahead to hire reporters, not journalism school graduates or people who had worked at other newspapers, but high school and college-age students who would work on a part-time basis. It was an idea I had suggested, but it was also something Doug had done earlier at the Democrat when he had hired a high school intern a couple of times. Even during the time since I had returned, we had used two people who were just out of high school, Martin "Bubs" Hohulin, a Liberal High School graduate, who later became a Missouri state representative and Penny Culp, a Lamar High School graduate.

Doug told me to hire students who were not involved in any extracurricular activities so they would have more time to the *Democrat*. I politely rejected that philosophy, telling Doug I wanted to hire students who were involved in everything. "Those are the kids who know how to budget their time."

I hired two Lamar High School seniors, Kari Wegener and Jason Stansberry, and a Golden City High School senior Peggy Brinkhoff, as our first reporters. The three high schoolers were not limited to covering school activities and stories for teens. Peggy's first story was a visit by Sen. John Danforth to the Horton Building in Lamar.

As the months passed, Kari and Peggy teamed to do an investigative series on city council members who also own businesses and the problems they have. The series won awards from the Missouri Press Association and the Kansas City Press Club.

Their success opened the door for other youngsters, From 1987 until I left the *Democrat* in March 1990, hard working, talented youngsters like Amy Lamb and Randee Kaiser (both of whom later worked for me at *The Carthage Press*) Holly Sundy, Cherie Thomas, Mindy Atnip, and Mary Lou Newman, worked for me, with Kari Wegener returning in the summer of 1988.

In July 1988, Kari and I teamed to provide the kind of story we had readers telling us they were surprised to see in a small town newspaper. It was not the tone of "Murder at the 71 Motel" that made it so unusual, but the scope and the breadth of the research that went into it, as well as the feature style of writing we used.

The article was about a 34-year-old man who took a 15-year-old girl from El Dorado Springs, Missouri, to a motel in nearby Nevada, where he had sex with her and then brutally strangled her.

I traced the history of the killer, while Kari interviewed people who knew the victim.

The story started with this chilling description, taken directly from a statement given by the killer to a Nevada police officer:

> *"I tied her hands behind her back pretty tight and let her lay there while I watched TV. I stuffed a sock in her mouth I originally planned to leave her, but I didn't figure on wasting her.*
>
> *I tied her up about 7 to 8 p.m. I tied her up with a cord I cut off the light by the bed up on the wall. I stripped a pillowcase, cut it a couple of times and used them around her mouth to hold the sock. She wasn't making any noise.*
>
> *I told her some things to scare the hell out of her, just idle threats at that time. All she had on at that time was a tan top and a purple top, two of them.*
>
> *I was thinking about my own life, not hers, crawling in my car and killing myself. Before I left work, I got a hose off a shop vac and took a piece of plastic pipe that I was going to kill myself with…"*

In my part of the story, I traced the killer's turbulent childhood, his problems with his domineering father, and his early brushes with the law.

Kari wrote about the teenage victim's rebellion against her strict upbringing as a Jehovah's Witness

> *"Back as early as fourth, fifth, and sixth grade," the woman said, "she would come to school telling stories about being pregnant and that she was going to live in*

*a big castle. Maybe if she had help then. The poor girl just had to think that way just to get away from her problems."*

The story continued, telling how the killer strangled the girl, then drank a few beers and watched a movie in the motel room before leaving.

Kari wrote the ending that stayed with people for a long time after they read the story, noting that the teenager's body was cremated in September 1986, the ashes were spread on the family farm, and later that day the family went on an outing to Worlds of Fun.

"Murder at the 71 Motel" received the investigative reporting award for weekly newspapers at the Kansas City Press Club Heart of America Awards the following year, the second straight year Kari, now 19, had won a plaque. She and Peggy Brinkhoff had won first place in general reporting the previous year.

With two or three youngsters and Judy Probert as my staff, we not only held circulation despite the price hike, we actually increased it.

The high school students I hired kept on performing at a far higher level than anyone could have anticipated. After the sparkling performance of Kari Wegener and Peggy Brinkhoff between 1986 and 1988, my latter years at the Democrat were dominated by the work of Amy Lamb and Holly Sundy.

Amy showed a knack for features, including one on twin Highway Patrol troopers who were retiring and another following up on a murder that shocked the people of Jerico Springs, a small town on the edge of our readership area.

Holly had a conversational tone to her writing that I put to full use, first by having her write a diary as a member of the Lamar High School volleyball team, and then when volleyball season ended, we converted it into a regular column, which ran each week in the Saturday edition. Naturally, we called it "Sundy on Saturday."

Sometimes her columns were light and silly, as you might expect from a high school student, but she also had an ability to pull at the heartstrings and three of her columns submitted as an entry in the annual Missouri Press Association Better Newspaper Contest enabled Holly to become the youngest person to ever win an award as a columnist in the competition. Her winning entry included her telling the heartbreaking story of the experience she had when she dressed in a Santa suit and went to a Lamar nursing home, a second column on the reaction of Lou Rix of Lamar to the death of her old friend, State Senator Richard Webster, and the thoughts of a South African exchange student about the turbulence in his country.

Holly also received attention when she was named the *Democrat's* sports editor early during her senior year in high school, the youngest person to hold that position at a Missouri newspaper.

*The Lamar Democrat* was so successful that Doug Davis decided to expand in 1989, adding a weekly newspaper in Jasper, a city 12 miles away, called the *Jasper County News*.

I covered Jasper City Council and Jasper R-5 Board of Education meetings for the new publication, while we also used coverage from Mindy Atnip, a Jasper High School senior, who covered school news, Cherie Thomas, a Liberal High School senior, who made weekly visits to the Jasper County Courthouse, and Holly Sundy, who wrote sports.

The *Jasper County News* was never too successful. It served mainly as a place for *Lamar Democrat* advertisers to extend their reach, and not many of them really cared about the Jasper market, since the city only had a population of about 1,200. The publication was finally shuttered in December 1990. By that time, I had been gone from the *Democrat* for nine months.

During my time at the *Democrat,* I had only considered changing jobs once- in 1986 when I talked with *Carthage Press*

Publisher Jim Farley and Managing Editor Neil Campbell about joining *The Press* as a general assignment reporter.

I started thinking about leaving the *Democrat* in early 1990. I had the feeling that I had about worn out my welcome with Doug Davis, and I was tired of making $250 a week.

So I called Neil Campbell, whom I had not talked to in four years and asked, "Do you guys still me want me at *The Press?*" which, in retrospect, really took a lot of nerve.

I could tell I had caught Neil off guard, but he surprised me by saying yes. One month later, I was the area reporter for *The Carthage Press*…making $250 a week.

# THE EARLY DAYS
# IN CARTHAGE

Thirteen years had passed since I had last worked at a daily newspaper and I was not expecting the transition to be smooth.

To make things worse, I was not planning on staying at *The Carthage Press* for any lengthy period. I was so ready to leave the *Democrat* that I took a job that paid me the exact same amount I had made in Lamar and making $250 a week when I was already 34 years old did not seem to be a sign of upward mobility.

For that reason, it took me a while to make the move to Carthage. For the first couple of months, I continued to live in Lamar. At one point, somewhat disenchanted with my new job, I even talked to Doug Davis about the possibility of returning to the *Democrat*.     For my first month at Carthage, I even moonlighted at the *Democrat*, writing stories for the graduation edition. Finally, I decided I could not take the step backward. For better or for worse, I had to totally leave the *Democrat* and I also had to leave Lamar. For financial reasons, I made a move that I did not want to make- I once again moved back in with my parents in Newtonia. That move made my early months at *The Press* even more difficult.

My duties were covering the area towns of Jasper, Sarcoxie, Webb City, Carterville, and to a lesser extent, Diamond and Lamar. I also backed up everyone else. If Pat Halvorsen, the city and courthouse reporter, was gone, I filled in for her. If the lifestyles editor Nancy Prater was not in that day, I took over her duties, including coverage of the Carthage R-9 school system.

When I joined the *Press* staff, I was the eighth member, something that seems hard to believe in these days 19 years later when the current *Press* staff stands at four.

In addition to Managing Editor Neil Campbell, Ms. Halvorsen, and Mrs. Prater, the staff included Sports Editor Kevin Keller, City Editor Jack Harshaw, reporter/columnist and former managing editor Marvin VanGilder, and photographer Catherine Ross.

I quickly realized that no one knew exactly what to do with me. It was a place that quickly drained my energy and, for the first time in my working life, I felt like I was just punching the time clock and filling in hours.

I arrived each morning at 7:30 a.m. or a few minutes earlier, and sometimes it would be an hour or more before I was given anything to do. And at that point, I was still trying to fit in and not sure how any aggressive moves would be appreciated.

I ended up spending about 12 hours a day at the *Press* building because it did not make sense financially or timewise to drive back to Newtonia, which was 30 miles away, and then return to Carthage for whatever event or activity I had been assigned to cover. So I found many different way to spend my time.

Sometimes I would read a book or magazines in the lounge area downstairs. Other times, I would go to the third floor and go through bound volumes of *The Press* to learn about Carthage's history, or I would look through the voluminous filing system set up by Marvin VanGilder. At that point, I was doing the extra reading just to pass time. Later, both as a reporter, and eventually as managing editor, the things I learned about the city's history would prove invaluable.

It did not take long for Neil Campbell to know he had a worker. If I were assigned to a city council or school board meeting, I would come back with a main story and one, sometimes even two sidebars.

It did not take long for me to realize that Neil was happy to see me turning in not only the stories he had assigned, but also a few extras of my own.

The big change as far as my status at *The Carthage Press* was concerned came in October 1990, only six months into the job. Though Webb City was part of my beat, it was primarily considered to be *Joplin Globe* territory. If someone from Webb City had an important story that needed to be told, it was a *Globe* reporter who would get the call.

And that's what happened when three Webb City Police officers beat up a man named Vince McCarty in the city jail following a routine arrest.

The story was delivered to *Globe* reporter Andy Ostmeyer and it was an explosive one. I was totally shut out of it and it probably would have remained so had I not received two lucky breaks.

The *Globe* changed its Webb City coverage and put Carol Stark, who received her start at *The Carthage Press*, on the beat. I have always felt Ostmeyer would have stuck with the McCarty beating and at best, I might have been able to keep up with him. Instead, the developments stemming from that beating became my story alone.

The second lucky break came when I was covering a Webb City Council meeting. When the council went into closed session to discuss a personnel matter, I hung around outside listening in on conversations. I have never been much at socializing.

During one of those conversations, I heard two people talking about the McCarty beating. A man said, "It sounds like they beat the hell out of him."

A woman responded, "You should hear the tape."

My time for listening was over. I managed to get a copy of the audiotape of the McCarty beating, get confirmation from an FBI source that it was looking into the matter, and that became my first major scoop at *The Press*.

After that, I followed it up with one story after another, developing sources on the city council and the police department.

At just about the same time, I filled in for Pat Halvorsen covering a hearing of the nationally known Nancy Cruzan right-to-die case.

As I noted in my earlier book, *The Turner Report*, I had known Nancy Cruzan, though not well, during my teenage years, and was saddened when I heard that she was in an automobile accident that left her in a persistent vegetative state, with no chance of recovery.

Nancy's parents, Joe and Joyce Cruzan, went all the way to the United States Supreme Court in an effort to remove the feeding tube, which was the only thing keeping Nancy alive. The court ruled that there was a right to die, but it did not necessarily apply to Nancy, unless it could be shown that was what she would have wanted.

The case was returned to Jasper County Circuit Court in Carthage and my coverage of the hearing, which combined the testimony coverage everyone else had, with a feature on Nancy's nieces, Miranda and Angie Yocum, brought considerable positive feedback for *The Press*.

Suddenly, I was being looked to as the go-to guy on the newspaper. When Sports Editor Kevin Keller left in late 1990, I asked to be moved into more sports coverage and then suggested to Neil Campbell that *The Press* take a different approach.

If I were to become a one-man night shift, I said, I could come in at about 1 p.m. each day, contact any sources who were only available in the daytime, and then cover meetings or help new Sports Editor Bill Denney, a newspaper novice who had two things on his resume that helped him get the job- he had been a Carthage Senior High School basketball standout, and as an aspiring actor, he had played one of J. R. Ewing's evil henchmen on a few episodes of the old TV series *Dallas*.

Neil readily agreed to the arrangement. It also made him feel more comfortable about assigning me to more nighttime events in Carthage.

It was a perfect arrangement for me. I had never been a morning person and now I could get to work at about 1 p.m., work until 1 or 1:30 the next morning, then drive home sleep late, and start all over again.

For Neil Campbell, it had to have been like having Christmas each morning. Unless he left me a message specifically assigning me to cover a meeting or an event, I was on my own. Whenever he arrived at work each morning, he would find one, two or even more page one stories on the computer, as well as some news briefs, and photo cutlines. He never knew what was going to be there, but nine times out of 10 there was something for that day's *Press*.

I made sure to have as many Carthage stories as possible, because I knew with my high volume of stories about Webb City, Jasper, Sarcoxie, Lamar, and the other towns I covered, a lack of balance could easily bring reader complaints.

The only problem I had with the readers during that time was the comparison of my coverage of Carthage High School volleyball and girls basketball to Bill Denney's coverage of Carthage High School boys basketball and football.

While Bill Denney, having no journalism experience, wrote stories filled with opinion and extensive play-by-play coverage, with little interviewing of coaches and no interviewing of players, and had an almost complete disdain of junior varsity, ninth grade, eighth grade, or girls' sports, I was offering game stories, features, and regular sports columns on the Carthage and area sports I was covering.

Bill happened to be at Webb City High School one night when I was covering a Carthage girls basketball game. Halfway through that game, a Carthage senior, upset with the coach, left the bench, went to the locker room, dressed, returned to the floor, strolled by Coach Ron Wallace and threw the uniform in his face, and then continued out the door.

When I wrote the story, I did not put in one word about the incident. Bill apparently put my story on the page without looking at it because he made no effort to edit my copy. However, once the paper was printed, he read it and when I came in at 1 p.m., he jumped all over me and said, "Conference room, now!"

I followed him and as we walked the short hallway between the newsroom and the conference room, I could see a look of fear in the eyes of the women who worked in the front office.

Bill Denney stood over six feet six inches tall and weighed close to 300 pounds, while I was slightly less than five feet nine inches and weighed around 165 pounds. The women were probably worried for my life, and to be honest with you, so was I.

"What the hell were you thinking?" he shouted, once the conference room door was closed.

I still had no clue what was going on. "What are you talking about, Bill?"

"When (she) threw her uniform at the coach, that was NEWS," he said, his voice booming even more than usual as he emphasized the last word.

"(She) is a high school senior," I said. "She is not being paid to play. She did not commit any crimes. Why should I put her temper tantrum in black and white forever? Someday her children and grandchildren would be able to see it. Those other girls stayed in the game and worked hard. They are the ones who deserve the attention."

Bill slammed his fist on the table. "Don't you understand? This is NEWS? We are in the business of printing NEWS, not hiding it."

On many occasions, I would agree with that sentiment, but not when it involved a high school girl. I tried, unsuccessfully, to reason with Bill. "If she had pulled a gun on the coach, then of course I would have reported it, but this was not a big deal."

That got him angrier. To Bill, it was a big deal.

As he was starting to shout at me some more, the conference door opened and the editor Neil Campbell stepped in, somewhat timidly. "What's going on, boys?" he asked.

Bill replied, "Well, let me just tell you about it." Without telling who was on what side, Bill outlined the situation, and then asked Neil, "What would you do in that situation?"

Neil hesitated, carefully thinking it over, then said, "I would have done exactly what you did, Bill. I wouldn't have mentioned the incident." It was the perfect thing to say.

Bill slammed his fist on the table again and stormed out of the room.

"I assume you were the one who kept it out of the paper," Neil said.

I nodded.

"Good."

Neil told me the women in the front office had called him in because they were afraid Bill was going to kill me.

After that, my job was ideal except for the growing tension with Bill Denney. Finally, one day he approached me in an uncharacteristically friendly way and asked me how I managed to turn in so many stories.

"There is no way you can write all of the things you write in 40 hours," he said.

And he was right. I had become extremely creative in filling out my timecards, always using different sets of hours, always making them add up to 40 since *The Press* did not want to pay, nor did it intend to pay, any overtime. But should I admit this to Bill? I took a chance and told him what I did. He was nodding his head the whole time I was talking. He thanked me for telling him and that was all there was to it.

Until two weeks later, when Bill Denney was fired. Publisher Jim Farley called me into his office shortly after Bill left the building for the final time.

He pulled a yellow time card out of his desk and all of a sudden I had a sinking feeling that maybe I was going to join Bill on the unemployment line.

Jim handed me the card. "Did you tell Bill to do this? He says you did."

I examined the card. On the front, the hours added up to 40. No problem there. "Turn the card over," Jim said.

I immediately saw the problem. Bill had written, "I put 40 hours on the front, but these are the hours I really worked." It was 65 hours.

"I didn't tell him to do that," I said.

"I didn't think so, but I had to ask."

And that was the end of Bill Denney's time at The Press. As Bill's replacement, Neil hired Randee Kaiser, who was going to graduate from the University of Missouri School of Journalism in December and who had worked for me at the *Lamar Democrat*.

And from that point on with Randee's skills at writing sports, editing, layout and photography, I could increase my coverage of Carthage and area sports, as I had with the regular news coverage.

We were moving closer to my goal of challenging the *Joplin Globe's* control of area readership.

My status at *The Press* was further cemented when we received word that the newspaper had won five awards in the annual Missouri Press Association Better Newspaper Contest. I was a bit embarrassed when I discovered I had won four of those awards- first place in investigative reporting and second place in coverage of government for the Webb City police investigation, second place in feature writing for the Nancy Cruzan story, and third place in sports column. We had also taken honorable mention in best coverage of young people.

When the MPA Awards Luncheon was held in Columbia, I paid for three guests to join me, Randee, who was his last weeks at the university, another School of Journalism student, Amy Lamb, and a student at Southwest Missouri State University in Springfield, Holly Sundy, all three of whom had worked for me at the *Democrat*.

I was hoping that the future of *The Carthage Press* would be established through the young people with whom I had worked at the *Democrat*, and for the most part, that is exactly what happened.

# THE TRANSITION FROM REPORTER TO EDITOR

During the next couple of years, *The Press* began its conversion into a legitimate competitor to the *Joplin Globe.* A series on the dangers of teen drinking, written by Nancy Prater, Randee Kaiser, our new city/courthouse reporter Glenita Browning, and me, received national recognition from Thomson Publishing, the newspaper's owner, as well as state and regional awards.

The weeklong series was the most ambitious project *The Press* had ever undertaken. It included interviews with law enforcement, school officials, and with teens, coupled with editorials on the subject.

I wrote the editorials and did a story on a young man in his late 20s who bought alcohol for teenage girls in exchange for sex. The story was based on numerous interviews with teens who told me about this man. Since he had never been charged with any crimes, I referred to him as "Bob."

That feature must have had a positive effect. A couple of weeks after it was printed, a man came up to me at a ballgame and asked if there was anything that could be done about Bob. Not that I know of, I said. I resisted the urge to call him "Bob," which was the name I had used for the same man who was talking to me, in the article.

The linchpin of our coverage was a freewheeling panel discussion with four Carthage Senior High School students. Lifestyles Editor Nancy Prater set up the interview and I recorded the discussion to help her with any quotes. As the discussion continued, I knew this was going much better than we had anticipated.

So while Nancy wrote an overall story about the panel discussion, I suggested to Neil Campbell that we take the recording, make a transcript of it, and print the entire thing.

Naturally, I was the one who ended up doing it. It took eight hours to transcribe the discussion, but it was well worth the time.

At the same time, as we were connecting with readers with the teen drinking series, my coverage of the problems in the Webb City Police Department continued to unearth one revelation after another, including the fact that the police chief had illegally provided machine guns to two of his officers.

Though it was obviously nowhere near the scale of the Watergate investigation, I was beginning to have some of the same fears that Bob Woodward and Carl Bernstein had as they unraveled the secrets in the executive branch. If my story was on the money, then why wasn't anyone else picking up on it? The *Globe* had carried little about the Webb City Police Department since the first story Andy Ostmeyer broke about the beating in the city jail.

The story was not being covered in the community's weekly newspaper, the *Webb City Sentinel,* and not a word had been mentioned on the three television stations serving the Joplin market.

Even worse, I was hearing that a *Globe* reporter had been criticizing my work, referring to it as being "mostly fiction" and had said, "Our editors would not let us get by with putting stories like that in our paper."

She was referring to my use of anonymous sources to detail certain portions of the story. Whenever possible, I named my sources, but in this case, there were people who were concerned for their jobs and for their physical safety.

Some of my reporting was backed by official documents, but they were documents that were not supposed to be public, and had been slipped to me by members of the City Council who were not happy with the way the police department (and the city) was being run.

I never featured a single item during my two dozen articles or so that could not either be backed up by two sources or by official documents. But still the *Globe* whispering campaign persisted.

I doubt if too many people were taking the talk seriously, but I was. I had worked too long and too hard to go from the miserable failure I had been at the *Newton County News* in 1977 and 1978 to being a good reporter and now I was being undermined.

It was a pattern that has continued for nearly two decades, a difference in the way the *Joplin Globe* (at least, the reporter who undercut me and who is now at the top of the *Globe's* food chain) and I approach journalism.

When Andy Ostmeyer broke the story of the Vince McCarty beating, I did not snipe at him and say that it wasn't a real story. I was determined to find a way to make that story my own through hard work and finding new sources. (And a little bit of luck did not hurt anything either.)

Whenever I broke stories at *The Carthage Press* or later on my blog, *The Turner Report*, instead of following up on those stories and making them their own, which would have been easy with the *Globe's* resources, the newspaper instead went out of its way to let it be known that my stories were not news after all. (If they were news, the refrain goes, "we would have had them in the *Globe*.") Perhaps that works for the *Joplin Globe* and its editor, but it has done a great disservice to the *Globe's* readers.

At least on the Webb City investigation, I was vindicated in a highly public forum, and in such a way that the *Globe* and the local television stations had to present the same things I had been reporting for nearly two years.

Four other officers, who were accused by Mayor Phil Richardson of being insubordinate, had joined the three police officers who had beaten Vince McCarty in 1990 on the unemployment line.

The four men sued to get their jobs back, and during testimony in the lawsuit in U. S. District Court in Joplin, all of the things I had written about were entered into the record.

*Globe* readers found out for the first time what was old news to *Carthage Press* readers (though the same reporter who had given me problems treated the revelations as if they were something new and dramatic).

And that was the last time I worried about being the only one who was covering a story.

◆     ◆     ◆

Despite having 15 years of newspaper experience, I still lacked one quality that good reporters should have. During my years at the *Newton County News* and *Lamar Democrat*, I had almost no confidence in myself. I was a reporter who had failed horribly at my first job and had been my own editor right up until the time I left the *Democrat* to work for *The Carthage Press*.

I was not a journalism school graduate. I was a teacher who had been unable to land a position and had lucked into one newspaper job after another.

I was always looking over my shoulder, expecting someone to tell me that it was time for me to hit the road and that the newspaper was going to replace me with a real reporter.

For the first time, except for a short period at the *Newton County News* when Emery Styron had been my editor, my work had to go through other editors. Sometimes it was Neil Campbell, sometimes Marvin VanGilder or Jack Harshaw.

It was a learning process, and I was surprised to find out that I picked up quickly on what things they were looking for, and just as quickly how I could do those things without sacrificing my writing style.

My coverage of the Webb City police situation and the faith Jim Farley and Neil Campbell showed in me helped boost my confidence level. My success with the feature on Nancy Cruzan's nieces enabled me to see clearly that my path to success as a reporter was not in following what others were doing, but to trust my instincts.

I kept doing things that were not being done at other newspapers, and for the first time, I did not worry about the wisdom of my solo flights.

I began digging up stories from court records that other reporters either did not have the time or the inclination to examine.

When I covered a Lockwood R-1 Board of Education meeting in which the superintendent's job was on the line, I listened through the paper thin library walls during a closed session that began at 11 p.m. and ended at 3 a.m., as the board asked the superintendent how much of a payment she would need to give up the final year of her contract. "You'll have to pay me the whole thing," she said. It was in *The Carthage Press* the next day.

I used the same technique at a Jasper City Council meeting when Mayor Fred Youngblood began shouting at council members during a closed session and I could clearly hear every word at my location in front of City Hall. When Youngblood confronted me before the next council meeting, saying, "I could sue you for writing about what goes on during closed session," Jasper's city attorney, Tom Klinginsmith, stepped between us and said, "No, Fred, you can't. You need to be a little quieter during closed sessions."

In sports coverage, I expanded what *The Press* was doing, by writing a regular column two or three times a week during football, volleyball, and basketball seasons, in which I did features on the players, sometimes having little to do with sports, but offering insight on the young athletes. It was something I started at the *Lamar Democrat* and by the time I left the newspaper business, I had written well over 1,000 Sports Talk columns.

I had almost no life except *The Carthage Press*, but I was enjoying what I was doing.

The most fun I had during those days probably came in 1992, when I became the *Press'* political reporter. It was the right time to move into that job since one of the major candidates for governor of Missouri was Attorney General Bill Webster, a Carthage native.

I can thank my former sports reporter and photographer from the *Lamar Democrat,* Martin "Bubs" Hohulin, for putting me on Neil Campbell's radar as a political reporter.

I gave Bubs his start in politics by having him write a column for the *Democrat*. When his columns received a warm response from the readers, Bubs decided to take on the herculean task of challenging six-term veteran Jerry Burch, a Democrat, for a seat in the Missouri House of Representatives.

At that time, the 126th District leaned toward the Democratic side, primarily because it included Vernon County. Bubs was a Barton County farmer and graduate of Liberal High School going against the smooth, polished Burch, who was considered a strong possibility for a run for lieutenant governor.

Almost no one took Hohulin's candidacy seriously, but I did. I noticed how hard he was working. Bubs was knocking on doors in every part of the 126th District. Burch was not. Bubs was hitting his opponent hard on his votes that seemed to be more in line with Kansas City and St. Louis interests than those of Burch's constituents in southwest Missouri.

Burch made the mistake many politicians make when they first start thinking about higher office. You will never get the chance to be elected to a higher office, if you don't take care of the people who are your constituents now. Hohulin found a receptive audience for that argument.

Plus, Hohulin had a catchy slogan, "No Foolin', Vote Hohulin," which he continued to use for the entire decade he served in the House.

Since the 126th District covered a portion of our reading area, I told Neil Campbell this would make a good story because Hohulin was going to upset Jerry Burch, Neil did not take me seriously, he told me later, but since I had been doing a good job, he decided to humor me and see what I could do with it.

I caught up with the Hohulin campaign at a rally at the Horton Building in Lamar on October 16, 1990. Almost immediately after Hohulin began speaking, he unveiled the proposal that turned out to be my first political scoop.

"I'm not going to promise you the moon," Hohulin said. "If I make a promise, I'll keep it." Shortly after that, he made a promise. He said if he were elected, he would accept a $2,800 raise state representatives were scheduled to receive in 1991, but that he would use that money to finance $350 scholarships for students in each of the eight high schools in his legislative district. The promise brought a huge round of applause from the approximately 100 people in the building. It was a promise Hohulin had put down in black and white on brochures that were handed out at the rally.

It was also illegal, something I knew immediately. When I returned to the *Press* office, a quick check of Missouri state statutes showed that candidates could not offer anything of value in exchange for a vote. The next morning, I called Steve Byers, director of the elections division at the Missouri secretary of state's office.

Byers said, "It sounds as if there may have been a violation of state election law." That was as close to gold as you are ever going to get interviewing a state bureaucrat.

When I called Hohulin, he said he was unaware of the law, which prohibited candidates from promising to donate to public or private interests any portion of their salaries.

Hohulin said giving up the $2,800 was not going to cause him any financial harm. "When you've lived on what I've had to live on, what these legislators make is unbelievable anyway."

Hohulin's stealth campaign to unseat Jerry Burch suddenly jumped to the forefront of state politics. It did not take long for my story to get picked up by the Associated Press and naturally, to come to the attention of Hohulin's opponents. And naturally, the Democrats blew it all out of proportion.

State Democratic Committee Chairman Eugene Bushmann described the scholarship promise as "a shameful political ploy or disregard for our state laws. It is a disgrace to try to get elected on the back of our young people.

"Jefferson City needs lawmakers, not lawbreakers."

For someone who was supposed to be politically savvy, Bushmann certainly played right into Hohulin's hands. What Hohulin did was an obvious violation of state law, but it was not a smart move to attack a politician who thought legislators made too much money and wanted to give some of it to needy students.

Hohulin defeated Jerry Burch in November 1990, soundly whipping him in Barton County and barely losing in the heavily Democratic Vernon County. Thus began the career of Jerry Burch, the lobbyist, who parlayed his dozen years in the House of Representatives to a long and successful career lobbying his former colleagues and their successors, a job that he has continued to this day.

Hohulin's victory one of the first of what turned out to be many success stories for the GOP during the next decade, a time in which the Republicans broke the Democrats' stranglehold on the Missouri Legislature to become the majority party.

Even after Hohulin was elected, his Democratic opponents would not let the scholarship matter go. Vernon County Prosecuting Attorney Neal Quitno (now a judge) filed criminal charges against Hohulin. Circuit Court Judge Mary Dickerson dismissed the case against him in June 1991, saying Hohulin's promise was protected speech under the First Amendment.

It did not end there. Hohulin's promise had to undergo scrutiny from the House Ethics Committee. Eventually, the entire matter was dropped.

As silly as that all seems in retrospect, the Hohulin story was the one that gave Neil Campbell the idea of making me the newspaper's political reporter. Because I had correctly tagged Hohulin as the winner in his House race, all of a sudden I was a savvy political expert.

Neil had already assigned me to one political story- the state senate race between Carthage lawyer James Spradling and the incumbent, Dr. Marvin Singleton.

Singleton had won a special election to fill out the unfinished term of Richard Webster, a longtime state legislator, former Speaker of the House, and one time candidate for lieutenant governor, who had died from cancer.

When Carthage radio station KDMO agreed to hold a forum between the candidates, I was there to cover it and that became my first opinion page column for *The Press* on August 4, 1990, even though that was not originally what it was supposed to be.

Since it was the only forum for the candidates, it also drew coverage from the local television stations. Singleton, as always, was nattily attired, and kept his suit jacket on at all times, while the rough-and-tumble Spradling slung his jacket across the back of his chair, rolled up his sleeves, and was ready for battle.

Singleton kept a large black notebook in front of him containing newspaper articles, statistics, and facts that he occasionally could inject into the conversation. Spradling carried only a wrinkled newspaper article outlining Dr. Singleton's views.

Those who only heard the debate on KDMO missed out on most of the fun. They did not get to see the smile playing at the corners of Dr. Singleton's lips when he thought Spradling was wrong, or the more theatrical Spradling, who sometimes rolled his eyes at Singleton's statements.

> *The only people in the studio, for the most part, were the candidates, station personnel and reporters from the area media. Outside, reminiscent of blues great Big Joe Turner's line about one-eyed cats peeping in a seafood store, was a small legion of Spradling supporters."*

The column was Neil Campbell's first exposure to my political reporting and I am not sure he was ready for my irreverence. Normally, the story would have been squarely on page one, but when he saw the previous paragraph and those observations, Neil moved it to the opinion page. It took a while for him to get used to my reporting style. It was the first time in his nearly two decades at *The Press* that he had come across this kind of reporting.

Some of my other observations from that debate:

> *Singleton, on the other hand, stressed his incumbency using the phrase "as your state senator" at least a half dozen times. He said he had "current" experience in legislation, an indirect reference to Spradling, who served as state director of revenue in the mid-1970s.*
>
> *Singleton made numerous references to bills that "we" had passed in the legislature, even though he was elected in a special election in June and the Legislature has not been in session since May.*

And this one:

*"When the forum ended, the two made eye contact for the first time, then shook hands with neither looking at the other. Spradling carefully folded the worn newspaper article and replaced it in his billfold.*

*The hour, like the campaign itself, had been a long one...both for the candidates and for the public.*

Singleton won the election but only by a handful of votes. In Carthage, Spradling dominated the incumbent, and he won Jasper County, but Spradling did not campaign in the other counties that made up the 32$^{nd}$ Senatorial District, while Singleton attended every community function he could go to until the first Tuesday after the first Monday in August.

After that, I referred to the senator as "Landslide Singleton," a moniker that stuck when he won re-election four years later, again by a razor-thin margin.

My approach to the Singleton-Spradling debate was the same one I used whenever I covered politics. Since the events I was covering often had already been on television and in the morning edition of the *Joplin Globe* before *The Press* was printed, I took a feature approach and it paid off.

When Bill Webster officially announced his candidacy at Missouri Southern State College, I told the story by watching the reaction of his mother, Janet Webster, who was sitting quietly on a metal folding chair in the middle of the room.

When Mel Carnahan made his only visit to Carthage in March of 1992, I interviewed him and covered his speech, but I added a sidebar on the difficulties Jasper County Democrats had with the logistics of getting the lieutenant governor to the Carthage restaurant where he met with the party faithful.

I also employed my sometimes quirky sense of humor and no one, including my editors, complained, so I kept on doing it. On one occasion, I took photos of the top three Republican gubernatorial candidates, the two Democratic candidates, and actress Rhea Perlman, the barmaid Carla from the situation comedy "Cheers" and showed them to people on the Carthage Square to see which one would be the most recognized. I fully expected the punch line to be that Rhea Perlman was the most recognized, yet more people recognized Secretary of State Roy Blunt. Rhea Perlman finished second, and Carthage native Bill Webster, on his home turf, could only muster a third place finish.

I also commissioned the first ever polls for *The Carthage Press*, driving down Garrison Avenue and counting the political signs. Naturally, I called it the Garrison Avenue Poll. With tongue planted firmly in cheek, I wrote about the candidates' mastery of "sign language" and treated the story as if it actually mattered.

And in a way, it did. Usually the candidates with the most signs were the ones with the most money, and as I have discovered countless times over the years, money is everything in politics.

As I noted in a chapter of my book, *The Turner Report*, one of the highlights of my coverage of the 1992 race for governor occurred on July 28, 1992:

> The primary was one week away and I spotted Secretary of State Roy Blunt heading into the studios of Lamar's new radio station KHST (the HST stands for Harry S Truman, Lamar's most famous native son).
>
> Blunt had become persona non grata in Carthage, due to a series of ads in which the secretary of state relentlessly attacked Bill Webster. The ads had helped Blunt narrow the margin and Webster's once seemingly insurmountable lead appeared to be in danger. The ad was one of the best attack ads Missouri politics has ever seen. It showed a carousel and gave the implication, later proven to be true, that Webster was shaking down lawyers for campaign contributions.
>
> I heard it said around Carthage, "Roy Blunt is going to pay for telling those lies about Bill Webster. When Bill's

*elected governor, Roy Blunt is going to be out of politics," or words to that effect.*

*But on that day in Lamar, Roy Blunt and his family were making the rounds, and had already been at the Democrat office. Roy was accompanied by his wife (at the time) Rosann, daughter Amy (now a registered federal lobbyist and a lawyer with the powerful Lathrop & Gage firm), and his fresh faced son Matt, barely in his 20s at that point.*

*Knowing that the biggest event in Republican politics, the Lincoln Ladies Ice Cream Social, was scheduled for that night at Memorial Hall in Carthage, I asked Blunt if he would be attending. "Are you going to go into the Tiger's den?" I said, a bad reference to Carthage's school nickname.*

*Blunt shook his head. "I don't think so. I don't think it would help me much to be there." He excused himself as the radio station's news director stepped out of his office. I waited with the Blunt family. Amy Blunt, a striking blonde, was talking with a radio station employee and young Matt was standing off to the side, looking out the window, and shifting from one foot to the other as he waited for his father to emerge from the studio.*

*I had a conversation with Rosann Blunt about everything from the campaign to the weather. She was one of Roy Blunt's biggest assets on the campaign trail. It surprised me to see the studio door open and see the secretary of state headed directly toward me. "You know, Randy, I think I will go into the tiger's den tonight."*

Considering that *The Carthage Press* was the only newspaper in the state of Missouri to endorse Bill Webster twice (the *Joplin Globe* was the only other newspaper to endorse him at all), it surprised some people when we portrayed Roy Blunt as a human being. That was not only the way I operated, but that was also something Neil Campbell expected.

And Blunt received his due in my coverage of the Lincoln Ladies Ice Cream Social. As I noted in my earlier book:

> *Finally, the door opened and a candidate for governor stepped in.*
>
> *It wasn't the right one.*
>
> *"What's he doing here?" a woman sitting a few feet from me asked, tapping the shoulder of a young blond woman standing in front of her when Roy Blunt walked into the room. It wasn't a suit and tie, button-down candidate who came to the ice cream social. Blunt was wearing a long-sleeved shirt and dark slacks, but no suit jacket, and looked more like someone on a Sunday stroll than a candidate for the most powerful position in Missouri state government. I glanced at the woman who asked the question. Naturally, she was wearing a Webster t-shirt and carrying a Bill Webster for Governor sign. I had spotted her handing out Webster campaign fliers earlier.*
>
> *The young woman responded, "Who?" clearly not having seen Blunt yet. As the woman pointed toward the door, the blonde's mouth dropped open, but she quickly collected herself. "Well, I'll say one thing for him.*
>
> *"He's got guts."*

I don't know if Roy Blunt picked up any extra votes from his appearance at Memorial Hall in Carthage, but it was a gutsy move, especially considering that this particular get-together was primarily a coronation for Bill Webster.

Again, from the earlier book:

> *Now that Roy Blunt was gone, it was time to get down to business.*
>
> *And that's when the lights went off.*
>
> *The strains of "Born in the USA" by Bruce Springsteen blared across the room. Everyone stood and the balloons*

*were released from the balcony, floating through the air in every direction. Bill Webster entered through the south doorway, a spotlight focused on him every inch of his trip. He began removing his blue suit jacket and as he walked down the aisle toward the stage, he tossed it into the audience. (One of his staff workers caught it.)*

*Webster made no effort to begin his speech. He stood at the front of Memorial Hall and basked in the adoration of his hometown. Those ladies in the 20s and 30s in their short, red, white, and blue cheerleader-type skirts were jumping up and down.*

*By this time, I had already been a reporter for more than 15 years, but I was still caught up in the excitement of the moment. No wonder we endorsed this guy twice. He's a superstar.*

My coverage of the Lincoln Ladies Ice Cream Social filled almost all of page one of the July 29, 1992, *Carthage Press*. After that, I was able to convince Neil to allow me to go to Jefferson City to cover the election night watch for Bill Webster's campaign. That turned out to be the beginning of the end for the Webster candidacy, which imploded as his Democratic opponent, Mel Carnahan, took advantage of the ethical allegations Roy Blunt had first leveled against Webster and won comfortably in November.

◆          ◆          ◆

As 1993 rolled around, Managing Editor Neil Campbell was absent more and more often as he dealt with numerous health issues. During the times he was absent, Marvin VanGilder and Jack Harshaw shared the leadership responsibilities.

By this time, our photographer, Catherine Ross, had left the newspaper, and when her replacement left after about a month, the new photographer was a University of Missouri School of Journalism graduate from South Dakota.

Ron Graber fit in well with Randee Kaiser and me, and right off the bat, won first place honors in two of the three photo categories in the MPA Better Newspaper Contest.

Toward the end of 1993, it was becoming obvious that change was on the horizon at *The Carthage Press*, but I had no idea what was going to happen. Our lifestyles editor, Nancy Prater, had left, and had been replaced by a woman who was clearly not suited for the position.

*The Joplin Globe* hired our city/courthouse reporter, Glenita Browning, and Neil was still not at the newspaper very often as his health problems worsened.

In October 1993, as I was going through files in our computer system, I noticed one on the almost never used 11/11/11 (everything was filed by the date) section, which was labeled "Managing Editor." Always on the lookout for new information, I read the first draft of a story detailing Neil Campbell's resignation as managing editor of *The Carthage Press*.

His replacement, the story said, would be *The Press'* area reporter, Randy Turner, and the remainder of the article detailed some of my journalism background.

To say I was stunned would be putting it mildly. And there was no one I could talk to about it since I was not supposed to have seen the article in the first place.

So I waited for someone to break the news to me, and waited, and waited, and waited. Days and then weeks passed and not a word had been mentioned. Neil was back in the newsroom and seemed to be doing fine. Obviously, his health had returned and the plans had changed, I thought.

About two months after I first read of my impending promotion, Publisher Jim Farley called me into his office. Neil was already in there. Jim did all of the talking and let me know that Neil was resigning for health reasons and that the managing editor position was being offered to me. My pay would go up considerably, he said, and the number he mentioned was much more than I was making.

"I don't want to just sit behind a desk," I said. "If I take this job, I want to continue to be a reporter."

Jim had no problem with that and a few moments later I discovered why. "You are going to have a five-man news staff and that includes you," he said.

The staff, in addition to me would be Randee Kaiser, Ron Graber, Jack Harshaw, and Amy Lamb. The last name came as a surprise to me. I had been pushing Neil to hire Amy, and she had sent her resume and clippings, but this was the first I heard about her being hired.

"What about Emily?" I said, referring to the woman who held the lifestyles editor position.

"When Amy is able to start work, we're going to let Emily go," Jim said.

I accepted the offer. It was decided to run two stories on the change. First, Ron would write a story on Neil's resignation after 19 years as managing editor and 23 years with *The Press*. There would be only a brief mention of who was going to take his place.

The article, which ran in the December 3, 1993, Press, was headlined, "Stop the presses...the end of an era."

Toward the end of the article, Neil said, "I'm very pleased that Randy Turner is going to take over. I've been a fan of his for a long time, long before he came here. He used to give me fits covering Jasper. He's really a terrific writer, and I know he's going to have a very successful career."

If that was not enough to swell my head, he continued in the next paragraph, "I think they (the readers) will be very pleasantly surprised because he's a natural. I think he has a calling for community newspapering, a real flair for it like no one I've ever seen. I've worked with a lot of talented people, don't misunderstand that, but I've never seen the same intensity and breadth that he brings to it. It's really amazing."

The article concluded with Neil saying, "It's been a good ride. I've really enjoyed my time here. It doesn't seem like 23 years. Four, five or 10 years maybe."

I did not quite make it to 23 years. My run ended at 22, but when I came across the article years later, I knew exactly what he meant. The 22 years had flown by.

# TAKING CHARGE OF
# THE NEWSROOM

For a short time after I became managing editor, we were working with a four-man staff, as we waited for Amy Lamb to graduate from MU.

In addition to Neil Campbell's resignation, Marvin VanGilder retired, leaving me, Ron Graber, Jack Harshaw, and Randee Kaiser to put out six papers a week.

For the first time in many years, Harshaw, *The Press'* longtime city editor, had to pound a beat. For years, he had pushed pages, doing the grunt work no one else wanted to do. He had taken care of the obituaries and putting out a weekly farm page. The only times he was in the field were when he was covering Carthage R-9 Board of Education and Carthage Rotary Club meetings. And that was a shame because Jack had a smooth, readable style, and was a stickler for grammatical accuracy.

With only five people, four until Amy arrived, Jack was back on the streets again...and he loved it. In the nearly four years I had been at *The Press*, though Jack was always friendly and helpful, he was in at 6:30 a.m., and gone by 4 p.m. He was putting in his time and did not appear to be enjoying himself doing it. Jack had been at *The Press* since graduating from the MU School of Journalism in 1951. For years, he covered sports, and after his promotion to city editor, he had spent just as many years chained to a desk Now he was covering the police department, City Hall, the Jasper County

Courthouse, and when he entered the newsroom each day, he was whistling, something I had never heard from Jack before.

◆          ◆          ◆

It would have been nice if I had a few weeks or months to ease into the managing editor position, but that was not the way things worked out.

It was only a few days after I was put in charge that an eight-year-old second grader at Hawthorne Elementary School, Douglas Ryan Ringler, was reported missing.

From the beginning, the Carthage Police Department figured the boy had been murdered and on Dec. 28, 1993, the same day Doug Ringler was reported missing, his body was found in a Kansas field, where it had been burned in an attempt to destroy evidence of a sexual assault.

We threw everything we had at the story, with Randee Kaiser and I writing stories, checking with the police department, the school, and any other source we could find. Jack Harshaw worked the regular police beat, and our publisher, Jim Farley, who was close friends with Police Chief Ed Ellefsen, was also able to come up with useful information.

It was only a short time before a friend of Doug Ringler's mother, Norma Ringler, was arrested for the crime.

After the arrest of Terry Cupp, I assigned *The Press'* newest staff member, Lifestyles Editor Amy Lamb, to cover the preliminary hearing.

Amy first worked for me at the *Lamar Democrat* as a 15-year-old high school junior. Since most juniors were at least 16 years old, I did not realize for quite a while that Amy's dad was driving her to her nighttime assignments. During her two years at the *Democrat,* she covered everything from school news to government meetings to a look back at a cold case murder.

Even at age 15, she was one of the best feature writers who ever worked for me. This was a perfect way to introduce Amy to *Press* readers.

Less than two weeks into her new job, Amy took over the story that had everyone in Carthage on edge and her gripping coverage of the testimony at the preliminary hearing, and her ability to add a feature writer's touch to courts coverage enabled her to offer the best version of the hearing.

Under the headline, "Mom, I'm sorry" spread across five columns, Amy's story, coupled with Ron Graber's black and white photo of Cupp being led into the Jasper County Courthouse by two deputies, covered the upper half of page one.

With Amy on board, I was willing to put our news staff, with five people, up against the staff of any small daily in Missouri. I was also prepared to compete against the *Joplin Globe*.

# NOTHING SUCCEEDS

# LIKE EXCESS

During those first few years as managing editor of *The Carthage Press*, I can't remember ever having a dull day. After being tested almost immediately with the Doug Ringler murder, our small staff put out the best small town daily newspaper in Missouri. I never had a doubt about that.

My only problem with being the man in charge was getting up early every morning. I was at my desk by 7:30 a.m., drawing up a page one dummy and writing whatever stories needed to be written.

On the rare days when we did not have a page one completely filled with local stories, we actually had news scavenger hunts. We would call on people on our beats, find out if anything was new, or follow up on old stories.

During those early days, I would set a time of 10 a.m., make sure we had someone pushing the inside pages to the composing room, and the rest of would hunt for stories. It was amazing how many times we came up with something that was not only newsworthy, but ended up being the lead story for the day.

And any Carthage event was played to the hilt. In the past, we had run a picture page for Carthage Senior High School's football and basketball homecoming games. After I took over, I saw no sense in not using the incredible talent I had at my disposal.

My motto at *The Carthage Press*, which I stressed to my staff, was "Nothing succeeds like excess."

A football homecoming game might have coverage by Randee Kaiser, a two-page photo spread by Ron Graber, and an interview with the homecoming royalty (Carthage had both a king and a queen) by Amy Lamb.

Ron was without a doubt the best photographer on a southwest Missouri daily and Randee Kaiser was not far behind him in the photography department, so I began giving them the go-ahead to run more pictures and larger ones.

Both of them loved to listen to the scanner and drop everything at a moment's notice to cover accidents, flood rescue situations, or anything else that might come up during the course of a day.

Randee turned around what had been a moribund Press sports page and made it a must-read. Ron, I found out quickly, did almost everything well. In addition to his photography skills, Ron was a wizard with the computer, had strong layout skills, and served as an assistant managing editor in everything except name.

When I was out of the office covering a story, Ron kept things running smoothly.

With all of their abilities, though, it was Amy Lamb who was the budding star on the *Press* firmament. She followed up her brilliant debut on the Terry Cupp preliminary hearing, with a string of powerful, award-winning features.

At my *Carthage Press*, the lifestyles editor did not attend club meetings and spend her entire day at elementary schools (though those things were important to a small town newspaper and received coverage). Lifestyles was a term that meant much, much more, and with Amy in that position, the lifestyles editor became the heart and soul of the newspaper.

Amy managed all of the staples of lifestyles coverage, the education pages, the weddings, engagements, and anniversaries on Saturdays, the food page with columnists Gardis Ohlson and Clyde Phillips (who was also our circulation manager) on Wednesdays.

The extra that Amy brought to us was the hard news feature. She showed signs of that skill with her coverage of the Cupp preliminary hearing, but that was only the beginning.

She continued her extraordinary coverage of the Ringler case with an award-winning story on the day that would have been the murdered child's ninth birthday.

In 1994, she shocked our readership with a powerful series on sex crimes, in which she went into a state prison and conducted an interview with a child molester, as well as interviews with law enforcement officials. "Crossing the Line" was a disturbing, but riveting masterpiece of reporting.

Amy also accompanied the Wampler family of Jasper to Potosi to cover the execution of one of the two men who murdered their parents, Harold and Melba Wampler.

Amy filed a news story on the execution and the following personal column:

Two guards stand in the outdoor courtyard outside the visiting room at the Potosi Correctional Center, both huddled around their radios. It's just after midnight Wednesday.

Soon after I walk outside where they are, they turn up the volume.

"So do they radio you guys when it's all over?" I ask.

"No, you hear the whole thing as it's happening," said the guard next to me.

I got a little closer and asked, "Where are they now?"

"They're in the second stage," he said.

"What's that?"

"It's the second drug."

Pancronium bromide. It stops the respiratory system. It's 12:04 a.m.

It's extremely quiet now as I look at the guards and out over the concrete wall where my Diet Pepsi is resting. There's no movement anywhere.

A third guard had come out a few minutes earlier. He was manning the metal detector inside the doorway.

Now, the mouthpiece to his headset is pushed up. He leans against the wall in a corner of the concrete courtyard inside the prison.

He just stands there, staring at his watch through his glasses, concentrating on the seconds ticking by. The bright lights from around the prison yard illuminate the night, shining brightly off the security fences and coiled razor wire behind him.

"Operation complete."

It's 12:06 a.m. Richard Oxford is dead.

Four minutes and it was all over.

I was the only media person who covered the execution who wasn't a state's witness. The others had arranged to be witnesses before Oxford's previous June 12 execution date, and I didn't know until last week that I was going to get to go to Potosi this time.

The family of Harold and Melba Wampler, who Oxford was convicted of killing, came up to the visiting room, which served as a press room tonight, soon after the execution.

They were quiet and looked thoughtful. They had just watched a man die. The man who killed their mother and father, the man who shot them in the head and left them in the trunk of their car.

The man who laughed and smiled in the courtroom during his trial. The man who had raped and sodomized many times before. The man who had a criminal background spanning more than 20 years and had escaped from prison.

The man who laughed at their family with his dying breath.

This was not an easy time for them, but it brought closure.

Many of the family members who were there, Jeff Wampler of Carthage, Brenda Cornell of Lamar, Greg Wampler of Jasper, Pam Tague of Spokane, Wash., and their cousin Dee

Wampler, a Springfield defense attorney, wished it could have been more severe.

Brenda Cornell said something last week that really made me think when she talked about her parents' deaths.

"One of them had to be shot first. The other had to hear those shots," she said.

That has to be one of the most horrible things I can think of.

I'm not even married yet, but to think about witnessing my fiancée's brutal murder, that is sheer torture.

And to be locked in a trunk, bound and gagged, and hear and see some lunatic escaped convict put a bullet into the head of your spouse of so many years- I can't think of anything worse.

"He should've been locked in the trunk of a car and have to go 130 miles bound and gagged and lying there with someone he loves, wondering what's going to happen," said son Jeff Wampler.

Richard Oxford knew he was going to die, but he put himself in that situation. He put himself on death row. He blamed his behavior on a life of drug and alcohol abuse that stemmed from a lousy childhood.

Millions of children have not so perfect childhoods, but you have to choose which course you take. One course can take you out of it, and the other just leads you farther down a path of your own destruction.

*Or to death row.*

◆     ◆     ◆

For everything that Ron Graber could do well, there was unfortunately, one area in which he was not proficient. He was a horrible speller. And when he came to *The Press* in August 1992, he was just an average reporter.

Over the next few years, Ron worked hard enough that he was not only one of the top photographers in the state, but he also was an award-winning reporter.

Ron won awards for his feature writing and for investigative reporting. It was the latter that made Ron a hero with his family and friends from his hometown of Freeman, South Dakota.

It started in May 1995 when the Missouri Highway Patrol executed a search warrant on the offices of Conquest Labs on the Lamar square.

As I noted in my book, *The Turner Report*, Conquest Labs' owner, Patrick Dallas Graham, had bilked more than 500 investors out of $5 million, selling shares in his company that was supposed to have developed an AIDS vaccine out of hogs' blood.

Of course, there was no vaccine. Graham continued to collect money and use it to buy cars and homes for himself and his family.

Digging through court records and interviewing victims of previous Graham scans, I ran several stories about the man.

From *The Turner Report*:

> As my stories about Pat Graham began running in the pages of *The Carthage Press*, one staff member was paying close attention, though I did not realize it at the time.
>
> Finally one afternoon, photographer Ron Graber said, "There was a man named Pat Graham who ripped off a lot of people in my home town. I think this is the same guy."
>
> At the time, Ron had been at *The Press* for close to three years after graduating from the University of Missouri School of Journalism. His hometown was Freeman, South Dakota, a town I had seen in one of the lawsuits that had been filed against Graham in Barton

*County Circuit Court. After that conversation, it did not take long for us to determine without a doubt that the Pat Graham who ripped off Conquest Labs investors was the same man who had fleeced the residents of Freeman, South Dakota.*

*"Is there anything I can do on this story?" Ron asked.*

*"Find some information on Graham's time in South Dakota," I responded and Ron went to work. It wasn't hogs' blood that Graham was touting during his time in South Dakota, but fine dining.*

*Ron's investigation showed that on October 26, 1977, Graham held a groundbreaking ceremony for The Cornerstone, a Christian-themed restaurant in Freeman. Plans for the restaurant included several private dining rooms, a picturesque fountain, and a stage for live gospel music. By the time of the restaurant's grand opening in September 1978, Graham had left Freeman, owing local tradesmen more than $130,000. First National Bank officials, from whom Graham had borrowed money, filed a lawsuit claiming he owed them $173,766.31. A Denver, Colorado, restaurant supply company sued for $90,271.83. Others filed suit, but most did not, fearing they would end up paying their lawyers more than they would ever receive from Graham. Freeman businessman Orville Waltner told Ron exactly what he thought of Graham. "Those kind, they'll do it once and if they crawl out they'll turn around and do it again. If Graham can beat this one, he'll just do it again. He doesn't care whose money he's doing it with."*

Our Pat Graham stories lasted two years until Graham pleaded guilty in Barton County Circuit Court to fraud charges and was sentenced to 15 years in prison, filing legal actions every year in attempts to get an early release. It never happened. Graham died in prison.

The Pat Graham story was not Ron Graber's only foray into reporting by any means, but his writing was limited. His skills as a photographer, who piled up plaques for spot news, sports, and feature photos, were much too valuable to have him do much writing.

But Ron's determination to become a solid reporter, something that did not take him long, is something I will always remember.

◆    ◆    ◆

After serving as *The Press'* sports editor for three years, Randee Kaiser was ready for a challenge. After Jack Harshaw retired in December 1994, Randee asked for a shot at the city/courthouse beat, which included coverage of the police department.

I had no idea when I assigned Randee to cover the police, that he would eventually join the police department.

Randee turned around what had been the worst department at *The Press,* sports, and made it into a showplace section, bringing home the first place award for best sports section from the Missouri Press Association.

He also was an excellent photographer.

The most memorable story involving Randee took place on May 2, 1995, at a time when Randee was on vacation. Publisher Jim Farley called me at home and told me he had received a tip from his Carthage Police Department sources that two suspects in the Oklahoma City bombing were being arrested at the Kel-Lake Motel.

For once, as I noted in my book, *The Turner Report,* we had the advantage over the *Joplin Globe* and even the Joplin television stations. News normally did not happen at a time that was convenient for an afternoon newspaper. This time, we could go all out, prepare entire pages for extra coverage and blow the competition away.

Shortly after I arrived at the *Press* office, Ron Graber came in and I went over the game plan. Our new lifestyles editor, Mary Guccione, a former *Joplin Globe* reporter, who loved to horn her way into big stories, had the chance.

But in order to make my plan work, I needed our normal police beat reporter and I knew Randee, even though he was on vacation, would kill me if I did not call him in on the story.

The following passage comes from *The Turner Report*:

> *"You can't call him," Mary said. "He's on vacation."*
>
> *"If I don't call him, he's never going to forgive me. He'll want to be in on this one."*
>
> *When I called, his wife answered the phone and it appeared Randee was having a heck of a vacation. "He's fixing the roof," his wife said. She finally agreed to let me speak to him and either Randee's scoop instincts immediately went into overdrive or he really didn't want to spend his vacation working on the roof. I told him not to bother to come into the office. "Get out to the motel and work from there," I said. "Have you got your camera and film?"*
>
> *"Yeah."*

While Randee and Mary Guccione worked every angle at the Kel-Lake Motel, Ron and I made sure that everything was ready to get the newspaper out on time, or as close to that as we could.

The Kaiser-Guccione team worked effectively, interviewing everyone in sight. Again from *The Turner Report*:

> *This was an odd couple of reporting if ever one existed. Randee stood over six feet, with dark black hair and a fastidiously groomed mustache, while Mary, a woman in her late 20s, stood only four feet 11 on tiptoes, spoke with an energetic Alvin and the Chipmunks type*

*voice, and had an appearance of looking ready for the*
*junior prom.*

Mary phoned in when the police were ready to take
the two suspects, Robert Jacks and Gary Allen Land, to the
Carthage Police station. When the suspects arrived, *The Press*
had two photographers, Ron Graber and advertising salesman
Stewart Johnson there, along with me.

In the space of about six hours, we turned out an
impressive package of stories and photos. Randee's account
of the capture and a photo he took at the Kel-Lake Motel
were featured above the fold, and the rest of page one was also
devoted to the story.

We had four more stories and more photos on page three.
We blew everyone away.

It would have been nice if the story had actually been
worth it. The "suspects" turned out to be a pair of gentlemen
who were driving across the United States, primarily on old
Route 66, stopping at motels where they swigged beer, chowed
down on Pizza Hut's Bigfoot Pizza, and watched movies.

Nonetheless, it was an exciting time for *The Carthage*
*Press*, and who knows, it might have been one of the days
that eventually led to Randee Kaiser's departure from the
newspaper business.

Randee, who was fluent in Spanish, was wooed away
from us by the Carthage Police Department, which needed
bilingual officers to deal with the city's growing Hispanic
population. He never looked back and has worked his way to
being a captain in the department today.

◆     ◆     ◆

While Amy, Ron, Randee, and later Mary Guccione, sports
editor Brian Webster, and general assignment reporter Tricia
Gould, were turning out some of the strongest newspaper

writing southwest Missouri had ever seen, I was also doing my share of writing.

With my Sports Talk columns, I wrote features about athletes that went far beyond the fields, stadiums, and courts. Though most of them were centered around the sport and profiled student-athletes or coaches, I became notorious for writing features that had nothing to do with sports, except that the person who was being profiled was in some way connected with an athletic activity.

I was the first sportswriter in southwest Missouri to interview high school athletes on a regular basis. Most of my competitors conducted cursory interviews with coaches following the game, and then went back and wrote their stories.

I purposely took my sports reporting in a different direction, and from the feedback I received, the effort seemed to be much appreciated. Among the Sports Talks were the following stories:

— Jasper High School graduate and former Crowder College softball star Symonne Wilson talked about witnessing the death of one of her Crowder teammates.
— Carthage volleyball player Andrea Friesen on her adjustment moving from Nebraska to Missouri
— Webb City cheerleader Miranda Yocum remembered her aunt, Nancy Cruzan of the famed right-to-die case
— The death of star Diamond High School, and former Webb City High School, athlete Kelli Dorsey
— Carthage High School football player Shaine Sundy, who survived a near death accident when he was seven to become an all-star
— The return of prayer to Lamar High School football games after threats from the American Civil Liberties Union
— The final game of Carthage High School standout volleyball player Tysha Lucas, as seen through the eyes of her mother, Peggy Lucas

The Sports Talk column began in the mid-1980s when I was at the *Lamar Democrat*, but really hit its stride from 1991 to 1999 with *The Press*.

Anyone who expected a normal sports column quickly discovered that Sports Talk was anything but. The following comes from one of my early *Carthage Press* columns, published on March 27, 1991, under the headline, "Ex-coach remembered":

> *Greg Kinser was in Illinois over the spring break when he heard the news.*
>
> *"I couldn't believe it. I was in total shock. This is the kind of thing that happens to somebody you don't know in Kansas City or New York. It doesn't happen to people you know."*
>
> *Kinser has coached the Lamar High School volleyball team to three district championships in his six years. Armando DeLaRosa was his assistant for four years.*
>
> *On March 15, DeLaRosa, who left teaching two years ago to study law at the University of Missouri-Columbia, hanged himself. He had murdered his wife only moments before."*

The column ended with Kinser wondering if there was anything he could have done to steer his friend back on the right path:

> *"I'd like to have five minutes to sit down with him and figure out what went wrong and why this had to happen.*
>
> *"Just five minutes."*

One of the Sports Talk columns that stayed with me the longest was a follow-up on a story that I wrote in 1995. In September 1998, I received a phone call from a woman in Lamar telling me that a special meeting was going to take place that afternoon at Lamar Elementary School. This is how I wrote about that meeting:

*Football coaches don't cry.*

*But you couldn't blame Alvin Elbert for getting a little misty. Two hours before his Seneca Indians played Lamar Friday night, the assistant coach met an old friend...for the first time.*

*Abby Phipps was in her prettiest dress and brought a football-shaped balloon with her as she prepared to meet the man whose letters have been eagerly anticipated at her home for the past two years.*

*The coach watched as the Phipps family's specially equipped van pulled up to the curb beside the Lamar Elementary School gymnasium. The side panel opened and Connie Phipps, eight-year-old Abby's mother, helped lower Abby's wheelchair to the street.*

*A smile crossed Alvin's face as he saw little Abby coming toward him, the football-shaped balloon tied to the arm of her wheelchair.*

*It was a little over three years ago, July 1, 1995, when the members of the Phipps family had their lives changed forever when a drunk driver, going in excess of 100 miles per hour, rammed into the back of their vehicle.*

*The accident killed Abby's eight-year-old sister, Julie, and left Abby and her father, Jerry, with permanent physical disabilities.*

*Through all of the pain and suffering she has gone through, Abby has never lost her smile and has been a source of inspiration for her family through the difficult times.*

*A year after the accident as Abby's family prepared for her sixth birthday, they organized a card shower for her. It was well publicized in area newspapers and one of those who read about the plan was Alvin Elbert.*

*"I teach a Sunday school class in Seneca," he said, "and when I heard about this little girl and what she had been through, I had my class send her cards."*

*After Abby celebrated her sixth birthday, Alvin's letters kept coming. "He has been wonderful," Connie Phipps said. "He's told us about his family and his farm and working on his house. Every time we get a letter from him, it brings a smile to Abby's face."*

*But until Friday night, the two had never met face-to-face. "She has been really excited about it," Connie said.*

*During telephone conversations, Connie had told Alvin about how he made Abby smile. "Now I'll be able to picture that smile," he said.*

*Alvin walked toward Abby, a big smile covering his face, and talked with her for a few minutes.*

*He bent down, gave her a hug and told her he would see her at the game.*

*The Phipps family is Lamar through and through, but on this particular evening there would be two members of the Tigers' archrival Seneca, team, Alvin and his daughter, Holly, a cheerleader, who would be the focus of their applause.*

*As the Phipps van pulled out, Alvin Elbert, still smiling, but with a trace of moisture evident beneath his eyes, said, "That's a great family. She's a great girl.*

*"Did you see that smile?"*

*We all know football coaches don't cry. It must have been the humidity.*

◆          ◆          ◆

# THE LAMAR PRESS

During slightly more than two decades in journalism, I was involved with three newspapers that went out of business, two of them with me as the editor.

I was the editor of the *Lockwood Luminary-Golden City Herald* when it published its final edition in October 1979. Ten years later, Doug Davis tried unsuccessfully to build an audience in Jasper with the *Jasper County News*, which survived my departure from the *Lamar Democrat* by only eight months.

I was more sentimental about Lockwood than I was about the *Luminary-Herald*, and I never cared much for the *Jasper County News*.

The third newspaper that went out of business, *The Lamar Press*, was an entirely different matter.

It was generally assumed that *The Lamar Press* was my idea. That was not the case. *Carthage Press* advertising saleswoman Becky VanGilder thought a competitor for the *Democrat* would succeed.

Not only did I not come up with the idea, I was totally against it. We had made strong in-roads in Lamar and I was afraid *The Lamar Press* would be a step backward.

Still, by the time Becky and Publisher Jim Farley talked me into it, I was convinced that it would be a success…and it was…at least artistically, for the 49 weeks it lasted.

As far as I am concerned, *The Lamar Press* is still the best weekly newspaper southwest Missouri has seen in the past quarter of a century. Once I bought into the concept, I started planning the content.

The keys, I quickly decided, were all local content, plenty of photos, strong school, sports, and courts coverage, and a stable of interesting local columnists.

*The Lamar Press* debuted on August 15, 1996, and was in the hole financially from the beginning. We made little effort to sell the concept to Lamar advertisers, preferring instead to offer Carthage advertisers a chance to reach new customers, something that did not seem to interest them.

We had copies of *The Press* thrown to nearly every home in Lamar, but failed to notice that the car was followed by people who picked up most of the newspapers before anyone ever had a chance to read them.

The first issue was filled with Lamar stories that had not been printed anywhere else, including a special multi-page section on the upcoming Lamar Free Fair, school features, an update on the Pat Graham fraud case and an introduction to the columnists who would be the heart and soul of the new newspaper:

— Lamar High School graduate Cait Purinton, who had worked for me at *The Press* and had begun her journalism career as a high school reporter for the *Lamar Democrat*

— Lamar R-1 School Nurse Nancy Hughes, a nationally known motivational speaker.

— 1993 Lamar High School graduate Katie Jeffries

— Marvin VanGilder, who wrote a column on Barton County history. VanGilder had begun his long and storied journalism career as a reporter for the *Lamar Republican* in 1940 at age 14 and had written the highly respected book, *The Story of Barton County*.

— Kim Stahl Earl, a 1987 Lamar High School graduate, with a knack for well-written columns featuring strong opinions.

Later, we added First Christian Church minister Doug Oakes, and food columnist Susan Davis-Mabe.

The people who read *The Lamar Press* loved it. Unfortunately, not many people could be counted in that number.

The first two issues were rock solid, but it was the third issue that was probably the best newspaper, word for word, that I was ever involved in publishing.

After it was published, Jim Farley called me into his office and said, "I hate to tell you this, Turner, because you'll let it go to your head, but this is one of the best damned papers I have ever seen."

It didn't to go to my head. It just made me determined to top it, though I was never able to manage that feat.

That third issue included Amy Lamb's column on the Wampler family as it awaited the execution of Richard Oxford, the man who killed Harold and Melba Wampler, an update on the Pat Graham fraud case, a report that claimed Barton County Memorial Hospital was charging high prices for its services, two full pages of Lamar Free Fair photos, two pages of photos from the Lamar Fair Baby Show, photos of new members of the Lamar R-1 faculty, two stories about Lamar High School student Ashlee Sorden, who addressed the National VFW Convention in Louisville, Kentucky, a Sports Talk column on former Lamar athlete Shannon Washburn, who was competing at Central Missouri State University, and a full page of records material.

The issue also featured columns by Amy Lamb, Nancy Hughes, Katie Jeffries, Cait Purinton, Marvin VanGilder, and Carthage Press intern Keegan Checkett, who wrote about her reaction as a stranger to the Lamar Fair.

The highlight of the newspaper, however, was a long feature about a Jasper woman, Cathy Bland, who did not know until she was an adult, that her real father was a Lamar war hero, Howard Layne, who died in Vietnam. I wrote about her trip to the Vietnam War Memorial in Washington to "visit" her father for the first time.

The article concluded with these words:

*In the middle of thousands of roses left by survivors for their loved ones who died overseas, there was one small Father's Day card in front of the section of the wall that contained the name of Howard Layne Jr.*

*"It was my first Father's Day with him," Cathy said. "And I do feel like he was there." In addition to the card, she wrote her father a letter, which she read to him as she stood in front of the wall. "I told him I was very proud of him for being in the war.*

*"And I told him he is not alone."*

*When she overcame her fear of heights to climb the ladder and touch the panel with her father's name, the torrent of emotion overwhelmed her. "I was really high up on that ladder. I started to rub his name off and it hit me hard. I started to cry." She began talking to her father once more. "At that moment, I knew I wasn't alone any more," she said.*

*"I grabbed the panel and I didn't want to let go of it. It was like I was hugging the wall and everything was better.*

*"It was so wonderful, so peaceful. I didn't want the day to end."*

Two days later, Cathy returned to the wall and said goodbye to the father who amazingly has become such a large part of her life more than a quarter of a century after his death.

"I said I'll be back next year and I will, I definitely will."

The visit to the Wall has answered a lot of unresolved questions for Cathy. Father's Day 1996, she said, "was the best day of my life. I know now that he loved me and that he is a part of me and that I'm a part of him.

"I'm proud to say, 'This is my dad.' "

When her son, John, who just began kindergarten last week at Jasper, is old enough to understand, Cathy says she will tell him about his grandfather. "I'll tell him he was a great war hero and he died for his country…and he died for his two little girls."

◆          ◆          ◆

My favorite *Lamar Press* story ran in the June 13, 1997, issue, toward the end of the newspaper's lifespan, but it was one that began more than four years earlier when I had an opportunity that most reporters never get- I covered the first kiss of a high school senior girl, and also captured it on film.

The story continued with a follow-up two years later in *The Carthage Press*. The final chapter, "Leigh Hughes: First kiss to lasting love," read like this:

> *Leigh Hughes received her first kiss in front of 1,500 people at the 1993 Lamar High School Basketball Homecoming.*
>
> *She received her wedding proposal in front of 1,500 people at the 1995 Lamar High School Basketball Homecoming.*
>
> *So naturally, when it came time for her to get married, she and her fiancée, Doug Kirkpatrick, exchanged their vows…in a traditional ceremony at the Lamar First Christian Church.*

## The Kiss

> *That first, special kiss is usually only recorded as a snapshot in the recesses of memory. More than 20 photographers captured Leigh Hughes' first kiss for posterity. Everyone knew it was her first kiss, thanks to her sister, Lindsay.*
>
> *The minute it was announced that Leigh was a basketball homecoming queen candidate, along with her senior classmates, Stacy Rice and Kristen Willhite, Lindsay served as her sister's unofficial campaign manager.*

*"I wanted Leigh to be the homecoming queen, because she's not just my sister. She's my friend and I love her.*

*"And I really wanted Brent to kiss her."*

*Lindsay was referring to LHS basketball player Brent Swearingen, who had been Leigh's best friend all through school. The younger Hughes sister let everyone know they should vote for her sister so she would be kissed for the first time.*

*"She embarrassed me to death," Leigh said, a few moments after the coronation ceremony.*

*When her name was announced as the 1993 basketball homecoming queen, her mouth fell open. "I just couldn't believe it."*

*She was crowned by Student Council President Melissa Main, then the shouts began.*

*"Lay one on her, Swear," one LHS student shouted in poor taste, encouraging Brent to give it his best shot.*

*Brent kissed Leigh. The crowd oohed and ahhed.*

*It was a pretty good kiss, Lindsay said, grading it an eight on a scale of one to 10. "It would have been a 10 if he had grabbed her and dipped her."*

*The kiss probably rated a point or two higher in Leigh's book. "It was a nice kiss," she said at the time. "It was a very nice kiss."*

*Of course, the kicker to that story was the other bit of information the wily Lindsay Hughes used to guarantee her sister's election.*

*She knew that the kiss was also the first for Brent Swearingen.*

*Though she didn't know it at the time, Lindsay Hughes' campaign set in motion a storybook four years for her older sister.*

## The Proposal

The romance of Leigh Hughes and Doug Kirkpatrick hit a snag on the day they celebrated their one year, five month anniversary.

It was the first time the two had argued. Doug, an Olathe, Kansas, resident, said the argument happened because he didn't plan to come to Lamar to celebrate that anniversary.

Actually, the argument was over nothing. Doug did plan to be in Lamar February 3, 1995. He just didn't want his girlfriend to know he was going to be there.

He had been looking for the perfect way to ask Leigh to share the rest of her life with him. They had fallen in love after meeting at a church camp, where they had served as counselors.

"(Leigh) always said that the best thing that happened to her in high school was when she was crowned homecoming queen and received her first kiss in front of the crowd and then the newspaper article was written about it," Doug said.

It was a very special night for her. I knew the homecoming was coming up, so I decided to see if I could ask her there."

The first thing he did was ask Leigh's parents, Leroy and Nancy Hughes, for permission to ask for their daughter's hand in marriage. After he received their blessing, he asked Nancy, who is the Lamar R-1 nurse, if the special proposal could be arranged.

It was okayed by Superintendent Barbara Burns and High School Principal Chuck Blaney with no problems, but it ran into a snag in the person of Athletic Director Dewey Pennell.

"He said Doug would have to get on the microphone and ask her to marry him so everybody could hear him *or he couldn't do it," Nancy Hughes said. Doug quickly agreed to the condition.*

*The next problem was getting Leigh to go to the basketball homecoming game. Once again, the catalyst was her baby sister, Lindsay. Lindsay talked her into going to the game and keeping her company.*

*The two had also talked about Doug, Lindsay said. "She said, 'I know he's going to ask me to marry him. I just don't know when.' I almost laughed my head off.*

*"I wanted to tell her so bad. We've always been close. I tell her everything."*

*So, on Friday, Feb. 3, 1995, Leigh, sitting in the bleachers on the east side of the LHS gymnasium, was surprised when public address announcer Ray Grissom asked her to come out of the audience. She didn't know what was going on, but thought it might have something to do with her being a past homecoming queen.*

*As she stood in front of the capacity crowd, she heard Ray Grissom say, "Here he comes."*

*Striding across the gymnasium was her boyfriend, carrying a bouquet of flowers.*

*"I was so happy when I saw him," she said.*

*Doug's hands were shaking slightly as he grasped the microphone, preparing to speak the most important words of his young life. Leigh was shaking all over.*

*Doug, speaking into the microphone, quickly recounted the story of how Leigh received her first kiss in front of the homecoming crowd. "I wish I would have been the one," he said.*

*He told her he planned to do "everything I can to see that you're happy for the rest of your life." He dropped to one knee and spoke from his heart, "Leigh, I love you. Will you marry me?"*

*His words came over the microphone loud and clear. Leigh did not give her answer over the microphone, but the smile on her face and the tender kiss that followed spoke volumes.*

## The Wedding

Lindsay Hughes didn't have to come up with any campaign slogans or use anything from her bag of tricks to get her sister and her fiancée to the First Christian Church Saturday.

Doug Kirkpatrick paced about the church anxiously as he waited for the ceremony to begin. He and Leigh had been together for only three years, nine months, and four days, but this was the moment for which he had waited a lifetime.

The families of both the bride and the bridegroom were seated. In a pew in the center of the church, another young couple enjoyed a chuckle or two as a slide show of pictures of Leigh and Doug from infancy on was showing.

When the slide show concluded, the wedding party came down the aisle. Then the wedding march was played. Everyone stood and Doug appeared totally overwhelmed when he saw his bride coming down the aisle on the arm of her father.

A few moments later, they exchanged vows, pledging their love to each other forever.

"One in name, one in aim, and I trust, one forever in God's name," minister Doug Oakes said. They shared a prayer, exchanged their first gifts, with each giving the other a red rose, then they were presented to the public as "Mr. and Mrs. Doug Kirkpatrick."

They walked down the aisle, watched attentively by the young couple in the middle pew, particularly by the young man. As they passed, a big smile was covering his face.

The Kirkpatricks stepped into the hallway with their family as the receiving line was formed. It took a *while, but the young couple worked its way to the front of the line.*

*Leigh Kirkpatrick jumped forward and hugged the young man as he offered her his congratulations. Leigh was standing beside the man with whom she plans to spend the rest of her life, but there's always a spot in a young woman's heart for that special childhood friend.*

*Especially when that friend is the young man who gave her her first kiss.*

Somehow, I have never figured out how, *The Lamar Press* kept going for nearly a year. We eventually reduced the size of each week's paper to eight pages, but even knowing that the end was near, I kept pushing. While *The Press* was being published, my 60 to 70 hours per week went up most weeks to 80 to 90. It was also pushing Ron Graber into considerable overtime since he designed the pages, while I provided most of the content.

Finally, Jim Farley gave me the word that American Publishing was pulling the plug on the Lamar newspaper. Initially the July 4, 1997, edition was scheduled to be the last, which would have given us no chance to put out a final edition. Jim gave me the go-ahead for a final issue and we went out in style, having a little morbid fun with the death of our newspaper.

The slogan we always put under *The Lamar Press* banner, "Barton County's Newest Newspaper," became "Barton County's Newest Dead Newspaper."

The lead headline read, "Last deadline met," with the kicker "Lamar Press goes the way of the Edsel." The page four jump to the story about the last edition was headlined "Lamar Press" Stick a fork in it."

But all was not fun and games with that last issue. We beat the *Lamar Democrat* on publication of the Lamar Free Fair schedule, featured my story, taken from Barton County Circuit Court records about the life of an undercover cop, final columns by Nancy Hughes and Marvin VanGilder, the only columnists whose work appeared in every edition, Cait Purinton, and our food columnist, Susan Davis-Mabe, and I even wrote a commemorative poem about a grudge tennis match between Lamar High School graduates Cait Purinton and Katie Jeffries (who by this time was selling advertising for us) and *Carthage Press* advertising salesman Stewart Johnson.

That last issue was Cait Purinton's chance to shine and the 19-year-old Kansas State University student made the most of it.

She wrote a column about her first car, and news stories about the Lamar Aquatic Park, an A+ grant for Lamar schools, and the Lamar Community Theater,

More importantly, Cait wrote four investigative stories about the Lamar Guest House, a troubled residential care facility. Cait's stories, which also ran in *The Carthage Press*, eventually led to the state of Missouri's decision to close the facility.

The page one story about the Guest House was headlined "Savage beating brings Guest House under state scrutiny" and caught the reader's attention from its first words:

> *Mitchell Henry was found in his room at the Lamar Guest House face down on the floor in a puddle of his own vomit June 9.*
> *His clothes were soaked with urine and his face was stuck to the floor with the dried vomit, according to Division of Aging inspection documents."*

The rest of that story and the others in the package were equally compelling. Cait wrote about problems the Guest House owners had with their facilities in other Missouri communities and revealed information that she had to supply to the Division of Aging which somehow failed to notice that the Guest House owners owed Barton County and the IRS back taxes, and had declared bankruptcy at one time, major problems since a state requirement to operate a residential care facility is financial solvency.

Except for our third issue, that final one is the best one we had put together. I hated to say goodbye to *The Lamar Press*, but I was also relieved. The pace was about to kill me and if the newspaper had lasted much longer, it may very well have done just that.

◆      ◆      ◆

Several months after the demise of *The Lamar Press*, the newspaper had one final hurrah at the annual Kansas City Press Club Heart of America Awards Banquet.

Cait Purinton was nominated for an award for investigative reporting for the Guest House series. I am claustrophobic and have extreme trouble driving in the big city, but there was no way I was going to miss Cait receiving her award.

Normally, I would have just hitched a ride with Cait, but she was staying with her sister, Colleen, in Kansas, and headed toward K. C. from the opposite direction.

I had no trouble getting to the site of the dinner and watched with pride as Cait accepted her award. When the banquet ended, I said my goodbyes to Cait and Colleen and headed to my car.

It was nearly 10 p.m. and a steady rain was falling, adding to my apprehension about the trip home. As it turned out, I had every reason to be apprehensive. Since I don't see well at night anyway and the rain made things worse, I turned where I thought I saw an exit and ran smack into a pole. I guess you could call it an "exit pole."

I stepped out of the car and checked it. I did not see any damage so I kept on driving, and soon realized I was hopelessly lost.

At one point, I found myself several miles into Kansas, but finally I made it home a little past three a.m. The next day,

I drove to Newtonia to see my parents and when I was ready to head home, I noticed I had a flat tire and severe damage to the wheel.

Somehow I had managed to drive my car more than 150 miles before my crash into the pole finally stopped me.

Having bad things happen on days that should be happy ones has always been a bad habit of mine.

# THE SALE OF THE CARTHAGE PRESS

In retrospect, the beginning of the end for me at *The Carthage Press* came when Thomson Newspapers sold the newspaper to American Publishing Company, the United States subsidiary of Hollinger International, a Canadian company.

Things were never the same after that. Jim Farley had been comfortable in his role as a Thomson publisher. He never had that same comfort after American took over. Much of his problem with the company came from his dislike of the Cope family, which managed this region of the United States for American. Kenneth Cope, the one-time publisher of the *Neosho Daily News*, was a top executive for American Publishing, while his son, Randy, who had succeeded him as publisher at Neosho, also served as regional manager.

While Jim had his problems with the Cope family, I also had my concerns. On two different occasions, I had been fired by Kenneth Cope's brother-in-law, Richard Bush, when I was working at the *Newton County News*, both times by mail.

On the other hand, I could see some possibilities of working with the *Neosho Daily News* to provide a serious challenge to the *Joplin Globe*. I mentioned the idea to Jim, but he let me know quickly that my ideas would not be received well by the new owners.

Jim's frustrations with his new bosses eventually led to his firing. The catalyst for his dismissal was the hiring of an office manager named Carolyn Baker.

Mrs. Baker, who was married to a Carthage police officer, embezzled at least $42,000 from *The Press*, something which Jim normally would have caught immediately except he was distracted by his difficulties with the new ownership. The theft was discovered by an internal company audit. Carolyn was fired April 24, 1997, and criminal charges were filed.

According to the police reports, Carolyn stole two checks and used them to close on a real estate deal. She took $41,000 from *The Press* to make a bank deposit, and then had the bank write a $40,580 cashier check to REMAX, a real estate firm, for Carolyn Baker/Carthage Press. After whiting out *The Carthage Press* from the check, she presented it to REMAX. At that point, she discovered she was still $2,000 short, so she used the same method on a check for that amount.

On February 2, 1998, Carolyn Baker pleaded guilty to stealing and Judge George Baldridge sentenced her to five years in prison, and then placed her on supervised probation, with the stipulation that she serve 90 days shock time in the Jasper County Jail. She was allowed to do that on 45 weekends. She also was required to pay back the money, which she did.

Naturally, we were surprised when Carolyn filed a suit in small claims court against *The Press*, seeking 80 hours of vacation pay and 50 hours of accumulated comp time.

The Press filed a countersuit against her.

In the lawsuit, she said, "As of this date, I have not been paid for the above mentioned vacation and comp time." She requested a subpoena for her 1996 and 1997 payroll records.

During a hearing, Judge Joseph Schoeberl asked, "Is this the case where there is an alleged misappropriation of funds? The Press' lawyer Stephen Carlton, now a Jasper County judge, said it was.

Carolyn did not say a word.

The judge did not throw out the case that day, but eventually Carolyn dropped the claim.

It was not long after Carolyn's arrest in 1997 that American Publishing showed Jim Farley the door and brought in his replacement, Ralph Bush, the nephew of the man who had fired me twice at the *Newton County News*, and also the nephew of top American executive Kenneth Cope and cousin of regional manager Randy Cope.

Other than growing up in a newspaper family (the Bush family owned the *Neosho Daily News* for nearly half a century before selling to American Publishing in the late 1980s, Bush had little practical newspaper experience. He had spent about two years running the national classified advertising network for American out of a Neosho office. From there, Ralph moved directly into the publisher position. And from that point on, even though I do not think that was what Ralph intended, *The Carthage Press*, with no Jim Farley to fight its battles, became the unwanted stepchild of the *Neosho Daily News*.

◆    ◆    ◆

The 1998 sale of The *Carthage Press*, *Neosho Daily News*, and other newspapers that belonged to American Publishing (a subsidiary of the Canadian company Hollinger) to the newly formed Liberty Group Publishing marked the start of a long period in which Hollinger CEO Conrad Black looted his company coffers, according to a report filed with the federal Securities Exchange Commission.

Most of American's community newspapers were sold to a California-based leveraged buyout firm, Leonard Green and Associates, for $310 million with $31 million going toward a "non-compete" clause.

What was never explained is why Hollinger should have been paid a non-compete clause when it is almost impossible to start a newspaper in a small community that already has one and make it financially successful. One of the selling points for these newspapers, which Liberty and its latest incarnation, GateHouse Media, have used to promote their newspapers to advertisers and investors, is that their newspapers are moneymaking machines because they have no competition.

As Hollinger continued to sell off the remainder of its community newspapers in the late 1990s and early this century, even more money went into these non-compete clauses, according to the report, and most of this money made its way into the personal bank accounts of Lord Black and two or three other high-ranking company officials. Buyers were also required to pay non-compete money to another publishing concern, which was totally owned by Lord Black and this handful of confederates.

The report indicates these robber barons took Hollinger for more than $400 million over a five –year period

Black was eventually sent to prison for his crimes. The breakup of American Publishing, however, led to the formation of the monolithic GateHouse Media, which gobbled up small town newspapers across the United States, stripped them bare as it did *The Carthage Press* and left them with only a tenuous connection to the local communities.

When American Publishing bought *The Carthage Press*, it was a stronger paper than the *Neosho Daily News*, with a better news staff, better advertising sales, and a solid printing business that included the *Webb City Sentinel*, the *Wise Buyer* (a Webb City shopper owned by the *Sentinel*), other weeklies, and nearly every high school newspaper in the area.

The company bought a brand new printing press, placed it at Neosho, shut down the printing operation in Carthage, sold our printing press, sent the print jobs to Neosho, where then-publisher Valerie Praytor scrapped nearly all of them, and forced us to have unrealistically early deadlines for an afternoon newspaper.

The dismantling of *The Carthage Press* continued over the years with the elimination of the inserters and the composing room, as everything except basic news and advertising positions, was farmed to Neosho.

Eventually, with nothing left to fill up the historic three-story building it had occupied for half a century, *The Press* was moved to a site that was more suitable for a fast food place. Not only was the new building unsuitable, but it also pulled The Press away from the center of the community, smack dab in the middle of a section that included the Jasper County Courthouse, Carthage Police Department, Carthage Public Library, Carthage Senior High School, and the Jasper County Sheriff's Department, and moved it away from the news.

Ron Graber, who was the paper's general manager at the time, made sure the voluminous filing system which had been so carefully constructed by Marvin VanGilder, and bound copies of *The Press* dating back to the 19th Century, were sent to the Courthouse Annex, in the original file cabinets, which brought Ron a stern rebuke from GateHouse Media officials since they had planned to dump the contents and sell the file cabinets.

In exchange for a few dollars, Liberty Group Publishing and later GateHouse Media tore the heart and soul out of *The Carthage Press.*

In the 10 years since I was fired, *The Carthage Press* circulation has dropped from approximately 5,000 to barely 2,000.

When GateHouse, unable to control Ron Graber, finally fired him two years ago, and Stewart Johnson retired, the only person left from my days at *The Press*, was John Hacker, who was in his third go-round. Hacker was named managing editor of the newspaper July 31, 2009.

Hopefully, John Hacker, who has done an outstanding job since his return to The Press in 2007, will be able to restore

*The Press* to its former high standing in the community, despite the best efforts of his bosses at GateHouse Media.

Incidentally, John's boss, the regional publisher for the GateHouse Media properties in Carthage, Neosho, Aurora, and Greenfield, is Rick Rogers, another reporter who originally was brought to *The Carthage Press* by me.

# RED OAK II

For the first several months after Ralph Bush took over as publisher of *The Carthage Press*, not much changed as far as the news department was concerned. I was beginning to think I might survive the Bush curse. The trouble started from a most unlikely source, a community from the 1930s that had been transplanted to rural Carthage.

The original town of Red Oak was located about 15 miles east of Carthage and by the time I came to *The Carthage Press* in 1990, it was just a memory.

But one Red Oak native never let that memory die. Artist Lowell Davis made his fortune with artwork depicting rural life, including a successful series of figurines. Davis became known as the Norman Rockwell of rural art.

His masterpiece may have been the reconstruction of the town where he was born. Red Oak had been a ghost town for decades, but Davis, who owned a large acreage outside of Carthage, decided to restore it.

Davis bought the original buildings and moved them from Red Oak to his land, called Foxfire Farm. And on Foxfire Farm, the restored community was christened Red Oak II. The community was described this way on its website:

> "Red Oak II included a Phillips 66 service station, an old schoolhouse, feed store, diner, town hall, jail, and several homes. Two buildings that were important in Davis' life are the blacksmith shop, where his great-grandfather once practiced his trade and the General Store that was run by Lowell's father and where he learned

102

*to sculpt and paint. Both buildings were moved from the original Red Oak townsite. Situated throughout the property are numerous Davis sculptures and old vehicles. Frozen in time, a walk through Red Oak II is a vivid stroll through the past."*

Red Oak II had been open from time to time over the previous decade, but it had only been open sporadically for a few years after a Jan. 17, 1995, fire at Lowell Davis' studio.

The Carthage Fire Department and Jasper County Sheriff's Department determined the fire had been deliberately set and a short time later Lowell Davis admitted he had done it.

As we reported in *The Carthage Press*, "The fire gutted the inside of the studio and ruined priceless unfinished paintings and sculptures, as well as contracts with Schmid Associates, a company with which Davis has been producing figurines for more than 16 years." Davis told *The Press* he "was becoming too proud" and said he "would never mass produce artwork with his name on it again."

We ran a letter from Lowell Davis about the subject in the Feb. 1, 1995, *Press*:

*"To my friends and neighbors in the Carthage area. I know there are rumors flying across the country in abundance, some true and some pretty far out. Therefore, I feel it necessary to tell you the truth in order to stop all the gossip. I cannot deny the fact that I did indeed burn down or at least gut my studio by fire, not to mention a few other off the wall things. I have to admit that the actions that I have taken were due to my burning the candle at both ends and were a result to my inability to function under the utmost stress and pressure.*

*"I just want to thank everyone of you who wrote to me in my time of need and who told me of their love and deep concern. Many of your letters brought tears to*

*my eyes and I have been totally overwhelmed with the amount of prayers directed my way."*

Davis said he was ready to get back to work and renew his dedication to Red Oak II, but over the next few years, little was done at the site and nothing appeared to be on the horizon until June 1998.

I had covered a few events at Red Oak II during my first few years at *The Press*, but I had not been there for a few years when staff photographer Ron Graber and I attended a Carthage Chamber of Commerce After Hours at a small rustic café called The Black Hen Restaurant on the Red Oak II property.

At this time, Red Oak II had not been open, but a Carthage native, Terry Reed, now living in Joplin, just 15 miles away, was taking over the property and the After Hours was being held there to reintroduce Reed to the community.

The Chamber's executive director, Heather Kelly, a tall, talkative redhead in her late 30s, introduced Ron and me to Reed and he quickly told us of the plans he had to restore the business to its former heights as a tourist attraction.

One of the first things he planned to do was to hold an event called the American Heritage Festival there on July 17, 18, and 19. The event would bring well-known patriotic speakers from across the United States and would also offer kiddie games and rides, Reed said. "It will be just like an old fashioned county fair."

Though it was a Chamber event and many of the men from the organization were dressed in shirtsleeves and ties (they probably would have had jackets, but it was a warm June evening), Reed's clothes were more in tune with the rustic setting.

Despite the heat, he wore a long-sleeved blue flannel shirt with dark jeans, looking more as if he had just finished a hard day's work on Foxfire Farm.

Reed, who was in his early 50s, was tall with salt-and-pepper hair, mustache, and beard. When he stepped to the microphone to address the roughly three dozen people who were shoehorned into the Black Hen Restaurant, his voice was folksy, but commanding. It was apparent that Terry Reed was no stranger to speaking in front of crowds.

Heather Kelly told me that Reed had written a bestselling book, and I filed that away for future reference, briefly mentioning it in my story and then I did not think about it again until quite a bit later.

The next day's *Carthage Press* featured a story about Reed's plans to transform Red Oak II and included a photo of Reed and an interview.

Reed said the renovations he and his wife were planning were designed "to bring to fruition Lowell and Charlie's dream (Charlie was Lowell Davis' wife) of turning Red Oak into a thriving, prosperous community while still maintaining it as a loving tribute to country values of a time gone by.

"People who come to Red Oak II have a chance to experience rural American values that seem to be vanishing."

It was another couple of weeks before someone working for him brought the agenda for the American Heritage Festival to the *Press* office.

After I read the list of speakers, I began to wonder just what kind of event was going to take place. The festival was billed as a way to "rekindle your patriotism," but these speakers did not fit my definition of patriotic.

However, the fun and games Reed described were prominently featured on the program. "Test your skills or simply sit back and chuckle," The games included a greased pig contest, sack races, tug o'war, goat ropin' (the G's must have been considered extraneous), arm wrestlin', canoe racin',, duelin', dunk tank, and bobbin' for apples.

This wasn't Red Oak II, I thought as I read the program; this was the Andy Griffith Show.

Part of the event was going to be held at Red Oak II, with the rest scheduled for the Precious Moments Convention Center. Precious Moments was the brainchild of another of Carthage's burgeoning community of artists, Sam Butcher, the creator of the bestselling Precious Moments figurines.

Butcher's Precious Moments chapel, with walls covered with his teardrop shaped characters portraying Biblical scenes, was, and is, one of the top tourist attractions in southwest Missouri.

Church services would be held at Red Oak's Salem Country Church with the message delivered by R. L. Beasley, a minister and host of a conservative talk show on a Joplin radio station.

Among the guest speakers lined up for the festival:

— Rep. Charles D. Key, a Republican state representative from Oklahoma, who was among the first to raise conspiracy theories about the April 19, 1995, Oklahoma City bombing. His speech was going to be on the "Oklahoma City Bombing Coverup," according to the program.

— Jim Lord, author of A Survival Guide for the Year 2000 Problem. The program said, "Mr. Lord believes that The Year 2000 Crisis will be 'the most dangerous and widespread technical calamity ever faced by mankind.'"

— Gary Webb, a former reporter for the *San Jose Mercury News*, who at one time had been part of a Pulitzer Prize winning series at that newspaper. Webb had left in disgrace after running a thinly sourced series that claimed the U. S. Government, primarily the CIA, was involved in selling crack cocaine in the inner city areas of Los Angeles to finance the Contras in Nicaragua.

— Author Chris Temple, a frequent contributor to far right wing magazines, would also address the Y2K bug.

— Joyce Riley would speak on how the U. S. Government was covering up the Gulf War Syndrome.
— Dr. Leonard Horowitz was author of the book, *Contaminated Vaccines, the Coming Plagues and Government Coverups*, and would address the possibility that the U. S. government may have planned the AIDS and the Ebola Virus.
— Col. Bo Gritz, described as "America's Most Decorated Green Beret" spoke of a connection between U. S. government and the heroin trade. Gritz was best known as the man who helped negotiate with Randy Weaver during the FBI's siege at Ruby Ridge.
— General Benton Partin would speak on "The Coming War of National Liberation and the Interdependence of Globalism and the New World Order...What Must We Do?"
— Hoppy Heidelburg, a former member of the grand jury investigating the Oklahoma City bombing. Heidelburg had been removed from the grand jury after asking the judge why the panel was not hearing certain witnesses or evidence. Heidelburg's topic "The Federal Government's Coverup of the Oklahoma City Bombing."

The largest segment in the program, not surprisingly, was devoted to Terry Reed:

*"Terry Reed was ahead of his time. In 1994, he co-authored the bestseller Compromised: Clinton, Bush and the CIA, an intelligence insider's first hand account which shocked the nation by exposing the Clinton Arkansas cabal as the ruthless and nefarious political machine he knew it to be. While interacting with Oliver North, Barry Seal, the CIA, and Arkansas' young governor, Reed saw Clinton as a reckless, yet calculated risk taker who shot craps with his political soul in an*

*attempt to leapfrog his way into the White House. Reed's book is now on audio tape, and is captured visually through his video documentary, The Mena Connection. His behind-the-scenes, eyewitness accounts of the tawdry and incestuous interaction of Arkansas power brokers and Asian influence peddlers who underwrote Bill Clinton's rise to power, nearly cost Reed his life. In simple terms, Reed became a liability who had to be silenced. Court documents prove an assassination attempt directed from the Arkansas governor's mansion was spearheaded by Bill Clinton's bodyguards. Reed's accounts of drug running, money laundering, womanizing and murder cast a bright light on the dark and secret life of Bill Clinton. Reed should know, he was in Arkansas with Bill Clinton when the Asian connection was made through Charlie Trie. Reed is convinced, as are other intelligence insiders, that foreign influences have 'purchased' our politicians. As a result, the American working class has been sold out through our one-sided trading policies that wink at human rights violations, gut America's industrial base, and if left unchecked, reduce the U. S. from a super power to a banana republic. Reed traveled as a spy to Mexico and saw first hand the massive transfer of classified technology to our trading enemies and incorporated his undercover footage from his video Vanishing Jobs. Hear Reed connect the dots of our leaders' treasonous acts that threaten the American dream. He will be speaking on 'CIA, Drugs and the Clinton Scandal from an Insider,' and 'The Sellout of America…Clinton and the Asian Connection.' "*

These speakers did not seem to be the kind I associated with a patriotic celebration. This appeared to be a who's who of the anti-government movement, and it did not take much internet research for me to get a confirmation on that theory.

I found most of these people on lists of speakers at Preparedness Expos across the U. S. Preparedness Expos started as soon as fears spread about the disastrous effects Y2K (the coming of the new millennium) would have on computer systems across the world.

The list of exhibitors for the American Heritage Festival dovetailed nicely with that speculation. Many were selling items designed to either help people prepare for Y2K or to frighten them because of what might happen when the time arrived.

The only thing that appeared to be different about these preparedness expos and the American Heritage Festival was the name.

I did not have a good feeling about what was coming to Carthage. My biggest concern was how *The Carthage Press* should cover the event.

# A STORM BREWING
# IN CARTHAGE

The more I found out about the American Heritage Festival, the less I liked the idea that the event was going to be held in Carthage. As the time for the festival approached, I was not seeing much advertising for it, either in our newspaper, or in other publications. I did not come across any television advertising, nor did I hear anything about the festival on the radio.

I received an anonymous phone call from a man who told me that the event was being heavily publicized in the Kansas City/Liberty/Independence area, and that he was hearing that Terry Reed was looking for investors and was going to turn Red Oak II into a survivalist compound. That did not seem far-fetched. After all, such places dotted the landscape in nearby northwest Arkansas and there was a militia-type compound in Vernon County, just two counties away from ours.

The publisher, Ralph Bush, was concerned about covering the event at all. "We would probably be better off just to stay away from it," he said.

I could see his point, but I did not agree with it. "If we are going to have thousands of people coming to Carthage, we have to have someone there," I said, and Ralph reluctantly agreed.

At the same time, word was beginning to spread around Carthage and the surrounding area about the nature of the American Heritage Festival. An effort was underway to warn people about the type of visitors that might attend the festival. Except for the anonymous call, and Ralph's concerns about the event, I had not heard directly from anyone, but an article in the daily Carthage newsletter, *The Mornin' Mail* on July 17, 1998, indicated Terry Reed was concerned that people might stay away.

The publication's editor, H. J. Johnson, interviewed Reed, who tried to set the record straight about the festival. "I've been a guest speaker at many of these (similar festivals)," Reed told Johnson.

"I've lectured in Cincinnati, Ohio. I've lectured at MYU, to students. Professors want their students in political science to hear stories, first hand experiences of government corruption and cover up. So there is an eagerness to find the truth or to find information that a lot of people feel the mainstream media doesn't bring to them."

At that point, the interview was doing nothing to reassure me about the nature of the American Heritage Festival. During the next portion of the interview, Reed stressed how much Carthage meant to him. "I had to get away from Carthage to realize how much I liked it." Reed said when he was younger he thought the rest of America was like Carthage, but he had found out that was not the case.

"I've felt some yearning over the last several years to get back to my roots. I don't know if that's a process of aging, or if it's truly some kind of a force bringing me back."

Reed continued, "To me, Carthage personifies – the old Carthage, not necessarily the Carthage now- but the old Carthage personified the rural American value system, to the square root. Very self-reliant, very detached from even the rest of Missouri. This was the little capital of this corner of this little Norman Rockwell setting that I was raised in. Red Oak II captures that nostalgic feeling for me and others. Lowell Davis has done a great job, whether it was intentional or not, of really recording history."

In the remainder of the interview, which was one of the longest stories H. J. Johnson had ever published in the *Mornin'*

*Mail*, Reed stressed how different the American Heritage Festival would be from the normal preparedness expos.

"Janis and I have been talking for a long time about our frustrations with these conventions that we attend. The constitutional conferences or whatever they may be- even third party conferences in St. Joseph or Dallas. They're no fun. Especially when they are not family oriented. They are gloom and doom, where people get together and complain and so diverse that you don't know how to use the information except go home and buy dried food and go to your basement. That's not what I want to do."

Reed said he wanted to "incorporate the best of all worlds," and have a Chautauqua type of event. Not too long after that statement, however, he was once again addressing his grievance with the U. S. government. "I'm getting tired of being beat up by my government, as an American. To hear the government tell it, we're illiterate, we're inferior, lazy, we can't compete, we're all drug abusers, we're all tobacco users. You know, after a while my government, all it tells me is the bad news. It has to have a 'war' on this and a 'war' on that. When's the last time you've heard the government say anything positive about Americans?"

Reed said he hoped to turn the American Heritage Festival into an annual "patriotic Woodstock." He told Johnson, "I point out when I lecture, Bill Clinton avoided the draft, was a hippy and a socialist, yet he's in the White House. I applaud him for what he did. He didn't fire a shot. He went underground, joined the system, and penetrated to the level that he took control, he and his group. We have to learn to do the same thing. If we disagree with the way government is functioning, what we have to learn to do is get as smart as it, and get back in it, not out of it. And learn to network and lobby like the big guys do. That's what I lecture on.

"Each one of the speakers at the American Heritage Festival, in one way or another, has paid a price for their stance or their lifestyle. And I admire people who pay the price. I like to think I paid the price in my own way."

The interview concluded with Reed telling Johnson about what Vietnam veteran Bo Gritz had sacrificed. "America's most decorated Vietnam veteran. I don't think anybody can question Bo Gritz' patriotism. And I've talked to him about this. He feels betrayed. He feels duped on why he served. We thought we were fighting, as soldiers, for the same value system that our parents fought for in World War II. That's a blurry line now. What's good and what's bad."

*The Mornin' Mail* interview did nothing to lessen my concerns about the festival. If Terry Reed really wanted to relieve Carthage residents from the doom and gloom of the Preparedness Expo speakers, he might have added a few who actually presented a different viewpoint.

Instead, his idea of lightening up the proceedings was to add a few kiddie games, and call the event a patriotic Woodstock.

And as all of this was going on, I received word that Jasper County law enforcement was preparing for the event. No one would be taking time off during the American Heritage Festival. They wanted to be prepared for anything.

# THE AMERICAN
# HERITAGE FESTIVAL

Growing more and more concerned about the speakers' list for the American Heritage Festival, I had to decide how to cover it. My staff was at the lowest point it had been since I had become managing editor in December 1993.

My lifestyles editor Amy Lamb Campbell, a University of Missouri School of Journalism graduate, who had worked for me all but a few months since January 1994, had left the newspaper to work at Wal-Mart's corporate headquarters in Bentonville, Arkansas. That was a powerful blow since Amy was one of the best feature writers in the state and had worked for me since she was a 15-year-old high school junior and I was editor of the *Lamar Democrat*. Amy had won numerous awards for feature writing and investigative reporting.

The miserly ways of our owners, Liberty Group Publishing, also ran off our talented sports editor, Brian Webster, who joined the sports staff of the Jacksonville, Illinois newspaper.

We were already down one position on the five-person staff (including me) that Liberty allowed us to have. That left our staff photographer and layout person, Ron Graber, who essentially served as assistant managing editor, and me.

Until we get the positions filled, and we wanted to wait until we got the right persons, Publisher Ralph Bush allowed me to hire a Carthage Senior High School graduate named Brooke Pyle, who had just completed her first year at William Jewell College in Liberty, for the summer. Brooke developed film and took pictures, and wrote occasional articles, though she was not comfortable with the writing aspect of the job. She had filled in the previous summer, so she was a known commodity.

Brooke, now a lawyer in Springfield, Missouri, was an excellent photographer, a hard worker, and someone who was willing to do whatever it took to get the job done.

Though I knew from the beginning it was not going to work out, we hired a man named Max Metsinger as sports editor. I could tell Max was not someone I was going to trust to do any reporting that was not sports-related. It did not take me long to realize he was not someone I trusted with any reporting that was sports-related.

I met the fifth member of the staff one spring day when I was invited to Webb City High School, about 10 miles from Carthage, by a counselor, to give seniors practice job interviews. The counselors hoped, and it often worked out that way, the interviewers would hire some of the students.

Jana Blankenship showed no signs of nervousness when she entered the small room that had been set up for the interviews. She introduced herself and when I asked her to tell me a little about herself, the traditional job interview icebreaker, she quickly reviewed her work for the high school newspaper, her love of writing, and hit me with a line that I had never heard before and have never heard since.

"I would clean the bathrooms to get this job."

We never had Jana clean the bathrooms, but she did get the job.

We also had another part-timer during the summer of 1998. Marla Hinkle, a Missouri Southern State College student, was brought in to help build pages, though she also covered news stories from time to time.

Our staff was so depleted that when the biggest sports event of the summer came, I specifically kept my sports editor out of the coverage.

During the week of June 15-19, the KOM Reunion was held bringing together minor league baseball players who had played on teams from Kansas, Oklahoma, and Missouri (hence KOM) in the late 1940s and early 1950s. The league had been based in Carthage during most of that time.

I had already seen enough of Max Metsinger's work to know there was no way I wanted to see him doing the kind of feature stories that this event cried out for.

So I assigned Max to cover the evening dinners, but when it came time to the major event of the reunion, an oldtimers baseball game for people who were in their late 60s, 70s, or even early 80s, I kept Max as far away as possible, telling him we needed to make sure he could cover the evening activities without getting into overtime.

Naturally, I used Ron Graber, the best photographer in southwest Missouri, to record the event for posterity. To supply the word portraits, I assigned Jana to do a feature on the oldtimers' wives and I would do the feature on the ballplayers and the game itself.

While we were at Carl Lewton Stadium, Marla Hinkle worked up a story on the effect the KOM Reunion was having on Carthage's economy.

The next day's paper was one of the few in which we had used full color, and it was the perfect day to do so. Underneath the headline, "The Boys of Summer," five columns across, we ran Ron's photo of the KOM Leaguers standing in the 90 degree heat, their hats over the hearts as the National Anthem was played.

Below that, Ron captured an action shot of Jumpin' Joe Pollack, a 77-year-old from Miami, Oklahoma, laying down a bunt, which he proceeded to beat out.

Jana's baseball wife story and my feature on the game, which coincidentally included an interview with Jumpin" Joe Pollack, were included in the page-one package, along with Marla's business story.

The only non-KOM story featured the news that Carthage Senior High School graduate, Dr. Janet Kavandi, an astronaut who was scheduled to take a space shuttle flight the next month, would be coming to Carthage for the annual Maple Leaf Festival in October.

One professional, Ron Graber, two inexperienced college students, one even more inexperienced newly minted high school graduate, and maybe the worst sports editor I had ever seen.

That was the staff I had when it came time for the American Heritage Festival. It should have been enough to handle it except for two things- Ron Graber was already over his 40 hours for the week and had to come in the next morning to lay out the Saturday paper and I had come down with some kind of summer virus and was as sick as I could remember being in years.

I showed up for work and made sure the Friday newspaper was put to bed, but after that I was ready to be put to bed. Though he was the only adult available, there was no way Max Metsinger was going to cover the festival, so that left the teenage girls, and I opted for Jana and Brooke to go to Red Oak II.

The next decision was which part of the festival to have them attend. Though my personal preference would have been to have covered the presentation of the former Pulitzer Prize-winning reporter Gary Webb, I decided on Oklahoma State Representative Charles Key, who believed the April 19, 1995, Oklahoma City bombing was part of a conspiracy that reached deep into the federal government.

Jana would handle the story; Brooke would take the pictures. After the assignments were made, I left for my apartment and slept for 12 hours straight.

At that point, I planned to cover Saturday's festival events, but I was still sick as could be. We would have coverage of the event from Brooke and Jana, so why did we need more? Why give more publicity to these folks from the Preparedness Expo circuit?

That was a decision that came back to haunt me.

# AND THOSE NUTS...

The next morning, I drove to a convenience store to pick up the Sunday *Kansas City Star*, something I did each week. After I returned to my apartment and started to read it, the first thing that caught my eye was a large color photo on page one of a man burning a flag. As I checked the caption, I realized the photo had been taken at the American Heritage Festival.

My first thought was that a half million people were reading about something that happened in my town and they were not getting their information from *The Carthage Press*.

I read the headline 'A PATRIOTIC WOODSTOCK' SPEECHES, EXHIBITS, CONSPIRACY THEORIES. This was all we needed- the big city newspaper was coming into little Carthage and making fun of it. This is what I had feared ever since I saw the list of "patriotic Americans" Terry Reed had assembled for the event.

The article confirmed my worst fears. Following the Carthage dateline, the article began:

> *"With the Precious Moments Convention Center as their staging ground, hundreds are gathering this weekend in this southwest Missouri town for a ``Patriotic Woodstock" with everything from greased pigs to conspiracy theories.*
>
> *Called the American Heritage Festival '98, the event - the first of its kind in Carthage - is drawing people from as far away as Florida and California. Estimates of the crowds Friday and Saturday ranged from 1,500 to 3,000.*

*About 70 exhibitors had booths in the Precious Moments center, selling everything from alternative medicine to survival gear. A few of them sold books such as The Militia Battle Manual and neo-Nazi and racist tracts.*

*The speaker list read like a ``who's who'' in the patriot movement, a loose confederation of groups that think government has overstepped its legal and constitutional boundaries.*

That was not so bad, but the article went downhill from there, with the worst paragraph, to my way of thinking, coming where reporter Judy Thomas wrote ``*You have at this event the conspiracies; you have Christian Identity; you have the speakers that are all the center of what's driving the Christian Patriot movement in the country,*" said Mike Reynolds of the Southern Poverty Law Center. "*What this shows is that the white Christian separatists have become well-established in rural southwest Missouri.* "

From what I had discovered, Terry Reed had not advertised the American Heritage Festival heavily in southwest Missouri, but Patriot movement strongholds, especially in the Kansas City/Liberty area had been swamped with ads. Most of the people who attended the weekend event had taken Highway 71 from Kansas City. Only a small number of curious locals had attended either venue.

All of a sudden, what had been a minor event that did not deserve much attention had become a black eye for Carthage. And there was no way I was going to let that go unchallenged.

I still was not feeling well Monday morning, but I dragged myself into work. Though the *Kansas City Star* did not have many readers in Carthage, word of the American Heritage Festival article had spread all over.

There was no way I could leave Jana's article as the only page one festival story.

The photos were another problem. We had absolutely no photos of any of the speakers. Brooke, quite correctly, knew that the better photos would come from the kiddie-type country fair games at Red Oak II and that was what we had. I selected a picture of kids riding in a miniature train called "Little Boxie."

Jana's story on Charles Key's speech was well written and captured his conspiracy mindset perfectly.

She concluded the story with this:

> *"Many people have been intimidated," Key said. "They have been told by the feds not to tell their story.*
>
> *"A lot of people don't want to think about the possibility of the government being involved because they fear for their personal safety."*

Jana's story was solid, but after the *Kansas City Star's* coverage, there was no way we could lead with that story. Somehow we had to have the Bo Gritz incident in *The Press.* So we used the Associated Press' version, which included some of the *Star's* coverage.

The AP story opened: *A chapel filled with the cherubic faces of Precious Moments figurines seemed an ill-fitting backdrop for tables strewn with survival gear and books like "The Militia Battle Manual."*

The description of Bo Gritz' burning of the U. N. flag was included in the article.

To complete the American Heritage Festival package, I interviewed Carthage Chamber of Commerce Executive Director Heather Kelly, who wanted to make sure the community was aware that the Chamber in no way supported the viewpoints of those who made presentations at the festival.

*Carthage Chamber of Commerce was not a sponsor or backer of the American Heritage Festival held here this weekend.*

*You wouldn't believe that if you were listening to talk radio shows this morning which were criticizing the Chamber for its participation in an event that had vendors selling Nazi literature and had one speaker, Bo Gritz, dramatically setting fire to the United Nations flag.*

*You wouldn't believe that if you read the Kansas City Star article that said the Chamber had a booth at the Precious Moments Convention Center during the Heritage Festival.*

*The Star article, written by staff writer Judy Thomas, which was the basis for the Associated Press article on page one of today's Carthage Press, also quoted Heather Kelly, Chamber of Commerce executive director, as telling the Star Friday that the Chamber was not backing the event.*

*"I do not recall at any time speaking with Judy Thomas of the Kansas City Star," Ms. Kelly said. "I did not speak with her." A review of Chamber telephone logs for last week showed no time in which Ms. Thomas ever spoke to anyone from the Chamber.*

*Ms. Kelly said the only conversations she has had with anyone representing the Kansas City Star were in regard to a Convention and Visitors Bureau seminar that was held over the weekend in Kansas City.*

*The Chamber was offered a booth at the Precious Moments Convention Center by festival organizer Terry Reed, Ms Kelly said, but did not accept the offer.*

*"We did not follow through with that," she said. "We did not have anyone there and we never told anyone we would have a booth there."*

*Apparently, the Kansas City Star reporter was going by the program printed by the festival's sponsors, which says the Chamber has a booth.*

*There was no booth set up by the Chamber or for the Chamber.*

*In the program, information from Chamber brochures was apparently used. It says, "American Heritage Festival visitors...Welcome to our town of Historic Treasures! Visitors to our city describe it as charming, quaint, historical, cultural, artsy, friendly and safe.*

*"We like those words and we work hard to keep it that way. For those of you who have not visited with us yet, come by our booth and let us tell you about the many things of interest in Carthage. Chances are, you'll like our town so much, you'll want to come back again and again...perhaps to stay"*

*"We did not even know we were listed in their program as an exhibitor until today," Ms. Kelly said.*

*The Chamber director said the organization's policy has never been to support particular political candidates or beliefs. "Our Chamber exists to support Carthage businesses," she said.*

*When our pages had been sent to Neosho to be printed, I began considering a follow-up to that day's coverage of the festival.*

After talking to a few of my sources, it became apparent that not only were the crowds not what Reed had anticipated, but most of the people who attended were not from the Carthage area.

Yet the *Star* article and the nationwide audience it reached through its inclusion in the Associated Press coverage as far as I was concerned had branded southwest Missouri as a teeming cesspool of white supremacists and conspiracy kooks. The more I thought about it, the more I knew I had to write a column addressing the *Star* reporter's assertions.

At the same time, I had to balance my reply in such a way that it would not alienate Terry Reed. Not only was he a Carthage native, but he was also the man who was going to turn Red Oak II into an even greater tourist attraction than it already was. That would mean big dollars for the community... and big dollars for *The Carthage Press*. Following the festival debacle, I did not think Reed was going to be able to make a go of it at Red Oak II, but I did not want him to be able to say *The Press* was the reason for that failure.

So I elected not to use Terry Reed's name in the column. I also had to make sure that I did not make it sound as if everyone who attended the festival was someone on the Southern Poverty Law Center's watch list.

So after three drafts, this was the column that ran on page four, the opinion page, of the Tuesday, July 21, 1998, *Carthage Press*:

### MANY APPEAR TO BE EXCLUDED
### FROM OUR AMERICAN HERITAGE

*A blanket of white descended last weekend over the rainbow quilt that is Carthage.*

*The American Heritage Festival brought with it many people who had well-considered, thought-provoking ideas. It also brought with it fringe elements who want to teach patriotic Americans the most efficient way to kill and who believe everything that happened in this country from the Oklahoma City bombing to Bill Buckner's error in the 1986 World Series is a result of a government conspiracy.*

*There were the Nazi sympathizers and other white supremacists. There were people who believe Armageddon is just around the corner.*

*They were here Friday; they were here Saturday; and the nuts were also sprinkled on our Sunday.*

*Carthage has its problems, just like any other city its size. Sometimes those problems involve racism.*

*But this is a community that has welcomed the Vietnamese, including the more than 40,000 who come each year for the annual Marian Days observance.*

*This is a community that has welcomed a large influx of Hispanics who have come here trying to capture the American dream.*

*This is a community that has made giant strides in overcoming the problems that have existed between blacks and whites.*

*When racial incidents have occurred in Carthage, such as the infamous mistaken identity situation last year in which eight Carthage whites beat a Hispanic man they believed had raped a friend of theirs, even though the man believed to be the actual culprit was already in custody- it wasn't just the Hispanic community that was appalled by the overt racism. We were all appalled.*

*When there is so much to celebrate in Carthage... and in the country...it is hard to understand how an event that calls itself the American Heritage Festival can be so blatantly one-sided in the part of the American Heritage it celebrates.*

*There are many, many problems with the United States government today, but let's face it, just how many governments allow the freedoms that permit an American Heritage Festival to take place?*

*We have freedom of speech. The First Amendment protects not only those who have a slight disagreement with our leaders, but those who advocate their violent overthrow. It also protects those who print manuals that give step-by-step instructions on how to maim, dismember, and kill.*

*This is a country that has always prided itself in allowing diverse viewpoints to be tolerated, heard, and on occasion transformed into movements that have changed the nation.*

*Thankfully, those ideas that have changed the nation have seldom been based on hate. The Susan B. Anthonys brought women the right to vote. A woman named Rosa Parks, by refusing to be shoved to the back of the bus, helped propel the civil rights movement. A convict named Clarence Gideon helped earn indigent defendants the right to counsel. The history books are filled with name after name of people whose ideas helped move the nation forward.*

*A number of people who participated in the American Heritage Festival in Carthage over the weekend have good ideas, ideas that could move this nation forward, but it's never going to happen as long as they align themselves with hate-filled profiteers who are willing to fan the flames of our greatest fears just to earn a few bucks.*

*The Nazi sympathizers and the white supremacists were here, side by side with the survivalists and those who see conspiracies behind every corner.*

*Those people were in Carthage.*

*Don't believe for one second that these people are Carthage.*

Over the next several days, I heard nothing but compliments about the column. Not one complaint was registered, not by Terry Reed, nor from any Carthage resident who had attended the festival.

No one ever called *The Press* demanding a retraction or a clarification. It became obvious the morning of July 27 that Terry Reed's plans of transforming Red Oak II were a thing of the past.

Lowell Davis stopped by *The Press* office and told me Red Oak II would not reopen and that he had no idea of the problems surrounding the American Heritage Festival. Mainly, Davis seemed tired.

"I'm a terrible businessman," he said. "I'm a good artist, a good husband, and a good father, but I am a terrible businessman." When he started Red Oak II, Davis said, "Everything was in mint condition. To see it all deteriorating is sad, but we knew we could never keep it up. It was taking more and more money to keep it open."

The attempt to sell Red Oak II to Reed and his group of investors had been designed to save his dream, Davis said. Now that appeared to be impossible. The interview with Davis ran in that afternoon's *Press*. After that, it seemed like the American Heritage Festival was a thing of the past. Unfortunately for me, that was not the case.

The first inkling I had that something was wrong came on a Saturday morning, Aug. 1, 1998. As I was driving to Joplin to do some shopping, I flipped through radio channels and on the local right-wing AM talk show of R. L. Beasley, who had been a speaker at the American Heritage Festival, I heard Terry Reed say he had filed a lawsuit against the liberal media who had damaged the festival. He mentioned the *Kansas City Star*, its reporter Judy Thomas, KMBZ Radio in Kansas City, a disc jockey at that station, and for a brief moment I prayed the libel suit was going to be limited to Kansas City, and then Terry Reed said the words, "*The Carthage Press* and its managing editor Randy Turner."

It wasn't much of a shopping trip. After about an hour, I returned to Carthage. Any hopes I had that *The Press* would at least be the first newspaper to have the story about the libel suit were dashed when I checked my answering machine and discovered a message from J. L. Griffin, a reporter for the *Joplin Globe*.

"Randy, I would like to get a comment from you about a libel suit Terry Reed has filed against you in federal court." He left a phone number for me to reach him. Though I hate to admit it, I had no thought of calling him.

Twenty-one years in the newspaper business. More than 30 regional, state and national awards for investigative reporting and not one time had anyone ever filed a libel suit against me. I had never even had a libel suit threatened for any of those investigative reports, but now I was going to be sued for a constitutionally protected opinion column?

I couldn't bring myself to talk to anyone about it. I walked the block and a half from my apartment to the *Press* office, turned on my computer and checked the AP wire. There was no mention of the lawsuit.

Since it was a Saturday, no one would be available at the court office. For a moment, I considered calling the publisher, Ralph Bush. I even picked up the phone and began to dial his number. Then I replaced the phone on the hook. I would just wait until Monday morning to talk to him.

I leafed through the pile of newspapers on my desk and found the July 20 paper. I read and reread the column. It was opinion and nothing in the column could possibly be construed as an unfair attack on Terry Reed.

In the past, when people had asked me how I kept from getting sued for the things I wrote about people, I always pointed out how I made sure I had two sources for every item I put in my investigative stories or I took it directly from documents. Even so, I always added, some day someone was going to sue me, because there is nothing to stop anyone from filing a frivolous lawsuit.

Though I said that, I never imagined a libel suit happening to me. Terry Reed was suing me and in the back of my mind, I had those same lingering doubts that all reporters have when legal action is taken against them.

Did I make a mistake? Did I miss something when I was writing about the American Heritage Festival? Perhaps it wasn't my column. Was it my interview with the Chamber of Commerce director? I pulled out the July 19 paper and scanned through that article. I saw nothing that would give Reed the basis for a lawsuit.

It had to be the column, I thought. And I would have to read about it in our top competitor's newspaper.

I couldn't eat anything that night and I did not get any sleep. When morning arrived, I walked to a convenience store, hoping the cool morning air would wake me up.

That plan failed since there is no cool morning air in August. I picked up the Sunday *Globe*, the *Kansas City Star*, and a soft drink, and returned to my apartment.

J. L. Griffin's story was on page two of the A section.

> *"Organizers of the recent American Heritage Festival at Carthage have filed a lawsuit in federal court at Kansas City seeking damages from local law enforcement agents and officeholders, alleging they portrayed the event as a gathering of extremists.*
>
> *They allege they also sustained damages because of the news coverage of two newspapers and a radio station that reported on the event.*

According to the lawsuit, Griffin wrote that Reed said several groups had elected not to participate because of rumors being circulated about the people who would be at the festival.

The event was going to be like a "Fourth of July celebration" the lawsuit said, until word spread that it would be attended by "terrorists, Ku Klux Klan members, wacko Nazis, white supremacists and separatists."

The defendants, in addition to me, *The Press*, the *Star*, and Judy Thomas were Jasper County Sheriff Bill Pierce, deputies Jerry Neil and Steve Weston, State Representative T. Mark Elliott, Presiding County Commissioner Danny Hensley, County Recorder Edie Swingle Neil, Mary O'Halloran of KMBZ in Kansas City, Knight-Ridder, the parent company of the *Star*, and Entertainment Communications, Inc., owner of KMBZ.

According to the article, Reed, his wife Janis, and a woman named Ann Funk of Belton, Missouri, who had been interviewed for the Star's story, were bringing the suit. Reed and his attorney, Todd A. Nielsen, described in the article as a "self-proclaimed conspiracy theorist," were attempting to have the suit certified as a class action saying that everyone who attended had been damaged.

I had only one consolation. I received a call later that night from a friend at the *Globe*, who related a newsroom conversation about the Reed lawsuit, involving the paper's editor, Edgar Simpson.

"Ed was pissed. He couldn't understand why you guys were getting sued and not us."

"If he wants it, he can have it."

# MONDAY MORNING
# COMING DOWN

Unfortunately, *the Joplin Globe* was not the only media outlet to let the world know *The Carthage Press* was being sued before we were able to put the information in our newspaper.

A four-page sheet called the *Mornin' Mail*, published by H. J. Johnson, had the scoop in its Monday morning edition, in a story headlined "American Heritage Festival Claims Millions in Damages."

H. J. Johnson left copies of the *Mornin" Mail* at coffee shops and stores all over Carthage. The sheet usually included some lame jokes, news from 100 years ago, and a folksy column "Just Jake Talkin' " written by H. J. He ran one news story per day, usually centered on a meeting of one of the Carthage City Council's many committees. The lawsuit story marked one of the few times H. J. jumped the story from page one to inside.

H. J. always referred to his publication as the only locally owned newspaper in Carthage. And he absolutely loved it whenever he had an opportunity to poke fun at the more established *Carthage Press*. The libel suit provided him with the perfect opportunity.

H. J.'s story left out most of the libel suit information concerning the public officials and concentrated on what the lawsuit alleged about *The Carthage Press*. From this source, I learned that Terry Reed and his attorney had carefully selected snippets of my column to make it appear far worse than it actually was.

Mary O'Halloran, Randy Turner, Entertainment Communications, Inc., and Liberty Group Missouri Holdings, Inc. were named as part of the class action requesting compensatory damages in the amount of $250 million and punitive damages in the amount of $500 million. The following is quoted from the document.

"On July 20, 1998, Defendant, Randy Turner, acting as Managing Editor for Defendant, Liberty Group Publishing, Inc., commonly known as Carthage Press, authored and caused to be published, two articles in the Carthage Press. In one of the articles authored by Mr. Turner in the Carthage Press on July 20, 1998, Mr. Turner brought to the public's attention, the fact that Judy Thomas had made false statements in her Kansas City Star article of July 19, 1998. For instance, Mr. Turner advised the public that the quotations in Ms. Thomas' article attributed to Carthage Chamber of Commerce executive, Heather Kelly, were absolutely false. The article also criticized statements made by Defendant, Mary O'Halloran, on her radio program of July 20, 1998. Ms. O'Halloran had attacked the local Chamber of Commerce. Nevertheless, with full knowledge that a portion of Ms. Thomas' article was false, Mr. Turner embellished upon the false assertions within Ms. Thomas' article which pertain to all of the Plaintiffs herein. Mr. Turner falsely stated in the July 20, 1998 issue of the Carthage Press:

'A blanket of white descended last weekend over the rainbow quilt, Carthage.'...

'There were the Nazi sympathizers and other white supremacists. . . They were here Friday. They were here Saturday and the nuts were also sprinkled in our Sunday.'. . .

'The Nazi sympathizers and the white supremacists were here, side by side with the survivalists and those who see conspiracies lurking behind every corner. These people were in Carthage.'

"Defendant, Randy Turner did not attend or observe any portion of 'The American Heritage Festival'. Upon information and belief, his entire article was based upon portions of a Kansas City Star article which he had already reported to be false in other respects. Defendant, Randy Turner and Liberty Group Publishing, Inc. printed the false statements above in willful, wanton, total and gross disregard for the truth."

And this was the basis for a libel suit? Everything I had printed was constitutionally protected opinion. Terry Reed had never once called to talk to me about any of this, and now he was suing me for $750 million and Liberty Group Publishing for a like amount...a $1.5 billion lawsuit!

The *Mornin' Mail* also included a statement issued by Terry and Janis Reed:

> *"It saddens us to say that we have been unable to solicit the cooperation of the Jasper County Sheriff's Office in setting the record straight about the American Heritage Festival, held July 17-19 in Carthage, Missouri. Due to political forces, a paranoid law enforcement bureaucracy, selfish interests within the Jasper County government and liberal media with an agenda, our festival was labeled a convention of 'white supremacists,' 'neo-nazis,' 'hate mongers' and, in general, an unpatriotic, un-American, antigovernment event. The American Heritage Festival was nothing of the sort and we would not have condoned such a gathering. We therefore regretfully announce that our only recourse to clear the air, clear our names, and remove the stigma for all those who attended the fun-filled and informative festival is to file suit."*

As it turned out, the *Mornin' Mail* not only beat us, but it beat us by a day and a half. At that point, U. S. District Court for the Western District of Missouri was putting some court documents on its website, but this was not one of them.

I contacted a friend at Associated Press to get us a copy of the lawsuit, but he was unable to get it until the afternoon. *The Carthage Press* and I were being sued for $1.5 billion, and we had already been beaten to the story by the radio station KFSB, the *Joplin Globe* and the *Mornin' Mail.*

The publisher, Ralph Bush, and I talked over how to handle the coverage of the lawsuit. Though we had added a new reporter, Jo Ellis, who had recently taken a buyout from the *Joplin Globe*, it was determined that I would write the story, but there would be no byline. Since Tuesday, Aug. 4, was also election day, we decided to run a Ron Graber photo of voting in Carthage at the top of page one, along with Jo's story about the city's Police Personnel and Administration Board's selection of Dennis Veach of Columbia to replace long-time Police Chief Ed Ellefsen, who had resigned to take a new position in Springfield.

The lawsuit story ran across the bottom of page one, covering all six columns. This is what I wrote:

> *Four Jasper County elected officials, the Kansas City Star, The Carthage Press and Press Managing Editor Randy Turner are among the defendants in a $5 billion plus lawsuit filed Friday in U. S. District Court, Kansas City, by American Heritage Festival organizers Terry and Janis Reed, and a Belton woman, Ann Funk, who attended the festival.*
>
> *The defendant list includes Sheriff William Pierce, 127th District State Representative T. Mark Elliott, Presiding Commissioner Danny Hensley, Recorder of Deeds Edie Swingle Neil, Chief Deputy Jerry Neil, Captain Steve Weston of the Jasper County Sheriff's Department, Mary O'Halloran of KMBZ Radio, Kansas City, Turner, Judy Thomas of the Kansas City Star, The Press, the Kansas City Star, and KMBZ Radio plus "John Doe and other unnamed defendants."*

The allegations made by the Reeds begin with information about their efforts to buy Red Oak II and to develop it into a "first class tourist attraction and residential development site.

"The Reeds incurred substantial costs in their pursuit of this expectancy," the petition reads. "Their plans were well known throughout the Carthage and Joplin communities, having received major favorable attention from the local media. By the week of June 20, 1998, all of the necessary agreements were in place, prepared and ready to be signed."

The announcement was made at a Chamber After Hours held June 18 at Red Oak II. At that time, the petition said, "Lowell and Charlene Davis announced to the communities of Joplin and Carthage through the local media their intentions of selling their property to the Reeds."

The petition then details the planning of the American Heritage Festival. "The Reeds invested large sums of money, immense time and effort in promoting this, the first tourist event as a 'kickoff' for all of their new development plans. The event received much publicity in Carthage, Joplin, and the nation as a whole.

"The American Heritage Festival was a family fun festival, much like a Fourth of July picnic celebration. It featured a dunk tank, greased pig chasing contests, train and pony rides for children, demonstrations of a one-man sawmill, an air show, speeches on subjects ranging from the Y2K computer problem to the Gulf War Syndrome, to combating new viruses and diseases.

"There were town hall meetings for the attendees to express opinions and there was a non-denominational religious service," the petition continues. "The attendees typically were normal, happy average American citizens, many enjoying their summer vacations. They were *nothing more and they were nothing less. Approximately 2,700 persons purchased tickets and attended the American Heritage Festival." Most of them were from the four-state area, the petition said.*

*The problems began for the festival, the petition said, when Rep. Elliott learned it would include a forum for local candidates. "Defendant T. Mark Elliott realized that his primary opponent (Steve Hunter) was associated with Terry Kent Reed. In an effort to destroy the reputation of a political opponent, Elliot set upon a course of conduct which included the solicitation of and enlistment of Jasper County Commissioner and defendant Danny Hensley, enlisted Hensley's assistance in contacting Sheriff William J. Pierce and concocting a plan with Sheriff Pierce to portray the American Heritage Festival as a breeding ground of terrorism, a Ku Klux Klan meeting, a convention of Christian Identity wackos, a collection of neo-Nazi sympathizers and, in general, a party for white supremacists and separatists.*

*None of them had any reason to say any of these things, the petition said. "The plan was to solicit the assistance of various Chambers of Commerce to get T. Mark Elliott re-elected. The plan included the portrayal of Elliott's opponent as a "right-wing wacko who believes in black helicopters."*

*On about July 13, the petition said, Pierce, Weston, and Neil were enlisted to "launch the assault."*

*Under Pierce's direction, the petition said, "Weston began researching the backgrounds of everyone who was going to be speaking at the American Heritage Festival on the internet. (He) dutifully gathered data and bits and pieces of hearsay and unsupported innuendo and rumor about some of the individual speakers from the internet.*

"Weston then began holding meetings with key members of the Jasper County government and influential citizens in the Joplin-Carthage communities. Among the individuals with whom he met with were Danny Hensley and Anna Ruth Crampton (Mrs. Crampton was an associate county commissioner.)

Weston told them there would be "criminal and anti-government elements" associated with the festival, the petition said. "During all of his presentations to various members of the local communities, he continually emphasized that he had files on all of the people involved with the festival. These were presented to the public as official investigative files of the Jasper County Sheriff's Department. Weston emphasized that the area was in imminent danger because the event would be attended by terrorists, Ku Klux Klan members, wacko Nazis, white supremacists, separatists, and the like. He even stated that abortion clinic bombers could be in attendance of the festival. Soon word spread through the Carthage and Joplin communities and surrounding areas like wildfire. All of the rumors suggested that there would soon be held a convention of white supremacists, Ku Klux Klanners, nazis and potential terrorists."

The petition indicates Hensley began contacting business associates of the Reeds. It says he got in touch with Lowell Davis and the owners of the land adjoining Red Oak II, R. Warren Kyte and Barney Scott, and told them that the Jasper County Sheriff's office had files indicating Terry Kent Reed is a "liar, a crook and he does not pay his bills." Hensley also told them that the festival would be an un-American, unpatriotic, anti-government event."

The petition says Hensley did this in an effort to stop the sale of Red Oak II and that it did cause Davis, Kyte, and Scott to back out of the deal.

*Edie Swingle Neil is being sued for actions she took as president of Carthage Chamber of Commerce, the petition indicates. She told Chamber Executive Director Heather Kelly of "the existence of 'voluminous intelligence files' in the possession of the Jasper County Sheriff's office, indicating that the American Heritage Festival was really going to be a meeting of the Ku Klux Klan. Up until that moment, the American Heritage Festival had the full support of the Carthage Chamber of Commerce. In fact, Ms. Kelly had endorsed the festival in writing. The Chamber of Commerce had even gone to the extent of setting up a booth at the location of the festival to promote the interests of the city of Carthage and its businesspersons. The Chamber of Commerce had gone so far as to pay for an advertisement in the program of the American Heritage Festival."*

*At that point, the petition said, the Chamber joined in "the drive to destroy the American Heritage Festival. (Mrs.) Neil had embellished her story with references to her husband. She claimed her information came from her husband and his 'official files.' (She) intended by her false statements to destroy (the) Reeds' kickoff event of their real estate development."*

*The petition says Jerry Neil contacted the Missouri Highway Patrol on July 14 "and advised them that there was imminent danger associated with the American Heritage Festival. At or about the same point in time, Sheriff Pierce contacted the Federal Bureau of Investigation, the federal Drug Enforcement Agency and the federal Bureau of Alcohol, Tobacco, and Firearms to advise them of the immediate and impending danger from the presence of hate groups associated with the festival."*

*Reed learned of the rumors that were circulating around Carthage from H. J. Johnson, owner of Heritage*

*Publishing Company and the publisher of a daily newsletter called the Mornin' Mail. "Johnson stated that he felt it would be in the best interests of the community if Reed were to permit Johnson to arrange a meeting between Reed and Neil to address the rumors. Reed agreed to travel to Carthage for the meeting and did so."*

*When he got there, the petition said, the attempts by the Mornin' Mail publisher to bring Reed and Neil together fell apart. "Johnson had placed a phone call to Neil, but Neil would not return the call."*

*Johnson then contacted Edie Swingle Neil to tell her about his problems getting in touch with her husband, the petition said. "(She" said she would immediately relay the message." Neil never got in touch with the Mornin' Mail publisher.*

*On July 14, the petition said, Reed was contacted by John J. Karriman, a former Joplin police officer who told him about the rumors that were going around. With Karriman's assistance, the petition said, Reed tried to get with Pierce and Neil "in an attempt to quash the rampant and vicious rumors circulating throughout Jasper County. Neil refused to meet with or talk to Terry Reed."*

The next day, the petition said, Pierce, Neil, and Weston hosted a meeting in the sheriff's office that was attended by representatives of the FBI, DEA, and ATF, in which they "conveyed the now widely-circulated false rumors."

The day before the festival began, "Neil contacted Sergeant John Howlett of the National Guard. Pierce was aware that the Missouri National Guard was setting up an exhibit to be displayed to vacationers at the American Heritage Festival." The petition indicates Neil said the festival was "a dangerous political gathering that could bring embarrassment to the National Guard. Neil further stated that the festival attendees had plans to heckle the guardsmen and degrade their uniforms. The sheriff's minion also falsely stated that the organizers of the festival had announced that the guardsmen were there to provide security. Soon after receipt of these false statements, the Missouri National Guard, under cover of dark, withdrew its exhibit."

Pierce then attempted to convince Jim Malcolm, chief executive officer of Precious Moments, Inc., to cancel its contract with the festival organizers, according to the petition. The FBI and DEA contacted Malcolm, with the same warnings, it added.

The same day, Neil told Lowell Davis that Davis "was in imminent danger because of his involvement with the American Heritage Festival. He asked Davis to place undercover agents at Red Oak II. Davis insisted that any officers or agents would have to be in uniform and have a high profile while on his property."

On the first day of the festival the other plaintiff in the lawsuit, Ann Funk, who according to the suit represents everyone who attended, arrived. "Very few people from the Jasper County/Carthage/Joplin area attended the festival. Upon information and belief, most of the citizens of the local area were bracing themselves for what they envisioned to be a second Waco experience near their own communities. Hensley was boasting "the reason there are so many people at the American Heritage Festival is because most of them are plain-clothed undercover agents."

The petition says Neil contacted the assistant superintendent of the Joplin R-8 School District and convinced him to keep the Joplin ROTC Color Guard and its cadets from participating in the 7:30 p.m. flag ceremony the first night of the festival.

The head of the ROTC unit, Major James Osborn, "informed Reed that the cadets would be withdrawn due to imminent and pending danger and what was perceived to be embarrassment that would be brought upon ROTC if it attended the festival. The cadet of the Joplin ROTC unit show who shared top cadet honors of the freshman class of 1998 is the son of Terry and Janis Reed," the petition said.

The place was filled with undercover agents, the petition said. "Agents of the Jasper County Sheriff's Department infiltrated the festival and harassed, photographed and cajoled attendees, hoping to disrupt and destroy the festival" and told them that if they stayed their lives would be in danger. Local citizens, as well as many attendees and exhibitors, fled the premises."

"With the exception of fear, danger, and paranoia caused by the defendants, the American Heritage Festival was a peaceful, joyful celebration of American heritage by typical American families from all over the United States. There were no arrests. There were no crimes reported. No nazis, white supremacists, white separatists, wackos of any type have been identified by any defendant or anyone else.

"The inability of the regiments of undercover armed agents present throughout the festival to make any arrests, indicates that no such individuals were in attendance at the festival."

In addition, the petition said, none of those undercover agents had a warrant or permission from the Reeds, who were leasing the properties at Precious Moments and Red Oak II.

The media problems began with an article written in the July 19 Kansas City Star by Judy Thomas. The article quoted Mike Reynolds of the Southern Poverty Law Center as saying, "You have at this event the conspiracies, the Christian Patriot movement in this country. What this shows is that the white Christian separatists have become well established in rural southwest Missouri."

The article also said *The Turner Diaries*, the book that was said to be the blueprint for the Oklahoma City bombing, was for sale at a booth. The article included a statement from Chamber Director Heather Kelly saying, "We've done what we can to accommodate them, but we are not sponsoring (the festival)."

Thomas quoted Reynolds although he was not at the event, the petition said. The Star also featured an article saying that at the Precious Moments Convention Center "a few of these right-wing patriots felt comfortable enough in this cutesy setting to put hatred for minorities and Jews on display and to peddle it to others. Welcome to the 1990s, where racism among us isn't just a whispered undercover thing."

Mary O'Halloran of KMBZ Radio "launched an all-out fallacious assault" on Reed and all who attended the festival, the petition said. She said, "The group that puts this out likes to call itself a patriotic movement, I myself say it is anything but patriotic, but dangerous, racist, anti-semitic, and neo-nazi."

Among other statements attributed to Ms. O'Halloran in the petition:

— "The organizers of the event were selling The Turner Diaries"
— "Terry Reed is the organizer of the event. If he doesn't like Mein Kampf, don't sell it, Terry."
— "I don't know that it was a festival about greased pigs. It was a festival promoting a point of view."

The petition says she "refused to allow Reed on the air," and even though her co-host, Jack Cashill, was at the festival, it did not allow him to speak.

The Press became involved with an article in the July 20 Carthage Press in which Turner quoted Ms. Kelly as saying she had never been in touch with the Kansas City Star to give them a quote. "Turner advised the public that the quotations in Ms. Thomas' article attributed to Kelly were absolutely false." The article also criticized the statements made by O'Halloran, the petition said.

"Despite saying the Star and KMBZ Radio reports were false, the petition said, Turner wrote in a column in the July

21 Carthage Press, 'A blanket of white descended last weekend over the rainbow quilt, Carthage.'

"He also wrote, 'There were the Nazi sympathizers and other white supremacists. They were here Friday. They were here Saturday and the nuts were sprinkled on our Sunday.'"

Also, "The Nazi sympathizers and the white supremacists were here, side by side with the survivalists and those who see conspiracies lurking behind every corner."

The petition notes that Turner did not attend the event.

In their first claim, the plaintiffs ask for $10 million each from Pierce, Elliott, Neil, Weston, Hensley, and Mrs. Neil for damaging the Reeds.

In the second claim, they ask for $10 million each in compensatory damages and $30 million each in punitive damages from each for causing the Reeds "pain, suffering, and humiliation."

The third claim asks for $10 million each in compensatory damages and $30 million each in punitive damages for damaging the Reeds' business.

The fourth claim says the county officials were acting in "a conspiracy" and in an unconstitutional manner and damaged their business. They once again ask for $10 million each in compensatory damages and $30 million each in punitive damages.

The same defendants are also named in the fifth claim, which charges them with destroying their business expectancy. The same amounts are named as in the first four counts.

The sixth claim, against Mary O'Halloran and KMBZ, charges slander and asks for $10 million each in compensatory and $30 million each in punitive damages.

The seventh claim charges that the county officials and Elliott inflicted "pain, suffering, humiliation and the chilling of their freedom of assembly" on Ms. Funk and everyone else who attended the festival. It asks for $250 million in compensatory damages and $500 million each in punitive damages against each defendant.

The eighth claim, also against the county officials and Elliott says they were responsible for "chilling their freedom of speech" and asks for $250 million in compensatory damages and $500 million in punitive damages against each defendant.

The ninth claim says the county officials and Elliott broached the freedom of religion of those attending the festival and asks for $250 million in compensatory damages and $500 million in punitive damages against each defendant.

> The 10$^{th}$ claim says the county officials and Elliott chilled exercise of the attendees' First Amendment freedoms and once again asks for $250 million in compensatory damages and $500 million in punitive damages against each defendant.
>
> The 11$^{th}$ claim, filed against Ms. O'Halloran, Turner, KMBZ, and The Carthage Press says those attending "suffered severe extreme emotional distress, humiliation, pain and suffering from the defamation of their characters" and asks for $250 million in compensatory damages and $500 million in punitive damages from each defendant.
>
> The 12$^{th}$ and final claim, filed against Pierce, Neil, and Weston, accuses them of "improper dissemination of investigative files" causing the Reeds, Funk and everyone else who attended the festival to "suffer pain, humiliation and embarrassment."
>
> It asks for $500 million from each of them plus attorney fees and costs.
>
> The plaintiffs are asking for a trial by jury.

It took more than two hours to write the article. After it was finished, I checked it over, and then Ralph Bush examined it. The last thing we wanted was to make a mistake. That was one reason we decided to stick with the court documents and not seek quotes from any of the county officials, either of the

Reeds, or even from Ralph, though it was tempting to offer a response when someone sues your newspaper and your editor for $1.5 billion.

As I pored over the court documents, I was still shocked to think something like this could happen. The wording of the petition sounded like something the speakers at the American Heritage Festival would say. Everything was a conspiracy directed at the Reeds to keep them from landing investors in Red Oak II.

That had not been my intention, but at this point that did not matter. This libel suit was not going to go away anytime soon.

# OUR RESPONSE TO
# THE LIBEL SUIT

It was clear that *The Carthage Press* had to respond to Terry Reed's lawsuit, but it was just as clear that I could not be the one to make that response.

So it fell to Ralph Bush. Ralph had only been publisher for about a year and in that time had done no writing.

For many *Press* readers, this would be their first introduction to Ralph.

The official response came on our editorial page on August 6, 1998, and was headlined "Press did its job in coverage of American Heritage Festival."

> *There has been a great deal of controversy over the American Heritage Festival that recently took place in Carthage. We have received a number of comments from people, some supportive of our coverage and some critical of our coverage. I want to make sure that our readers understand why we chose to run what we did.*
>
> *We are a Carthage newspaper and we have a responsibility to the citizens of Carthage to keep them informed about what is happening in their community.*
>
> *Contrary to what you may have heard, we DID have reporters at the festival along with several other papers. The Kansas City Star provided the story to the Associated Press, who then distributed it nationally. Yes, we could have reported only the pleasant parts to the*

*people of Carthage and left out the part that some people did not want to hear. We could have just pretended that all of these other papers weren't going to run the article. However, our readers look to us for the news in Carthage. Sometimes it is good news; sometimes it is unpleasant. Either way, I believe that we have a responsibility to our readers.*

*We also ran an editorial column by Randy Turner that was plainly marked as opinion. Since that time we have run letters to the editor by Janis Reed and several others that expressed opinions contrary to Randy's.*

*In fact, there has been almost twice as much space on our editorial page given to those that were opposed to our coverage.*

*The more I learn about Carthage, the more I am amazed at how much Carthage has to offer. People in Carthage have spent a tremendous amount of time and effort to let others know about all of the things that are in Carthage. It is unfortunate that Carthage will now be remembered for the controversy surrounding the festival. Would this situation have been prevented if The Carthage Press had not covered this event? No! It just means that people in the rest of the state would have heard about it but Carthage wouldn't.*

*As you have probably all heard, The Carthage Press has been named in a lawsuit along with several others. The suit names several county officials, our state representative and several other members of the media. As I look through the list of defendants, I keep thinking that I am in pretty good company.*

*Our criteria for news coverage is simple: what is best for the long term growth and well being of Carthage. I am sure we would have been criticized either way so I guess that I would rather be criticized for providing the community with too much news instead of not enough.*

We had received negative letters to the editor about our coverage of the American Heritage Festival, but only one of those, the one from Janis Reed, came from within Jasper County. I had the feeling that some of the writers had not read my actual column, except of course, for the snippets Reed used in the lawsuit.

For the next couple of days, I did my regular work during the daytime hours, but after the Press office closed at 5 p.m., I began surfing the internet for information on Terry Reed. I knew about his book, *Compromised, Clinton, Bush and the CIA*, I knew he was a 1966 graduate of Carthage Senior High School, but other than that, I really did not know much about the man.

It did not take me long to find out that this was not the first time he had been in court. He had a long history of lawsuits.

At different times, Reed had claimed that President Bill Clinton, key Clinton aides, Lt. Col. Oliver North, and an unspecified number of federal judges had all done things to get on Reed's bad side.

I found a transcript of a 1994 radio interview in which Reed spoke of his background. "I was a true baby boomer, born in 1948, raised in southwest Missouri, 21 miles from Harry Truman's birthplace and hometown, Lamar. I'm from Carthage, Missouri. I'm the youngest of six children, raised to be patriotic and serve my country. I did so."

Reed's earlier lawsuits were filed in connection with his claim that at one point he served his country as a CIA operative and had trained Contra pilots at a one-runway airport in Mena, Arkansas, a town with a population of about 5,500. Reed, both in his book and on conservative radio talk shows, said the Mena airport was used as a starting point for shipping arms to the Contras in exchange for drugs, something Reed said he was unaware of in the beginning and wanted no part of once he found out about it.

Reed said during the 1994 radio interview that then-Gov. Clinton was in on the scheme and that 10 percent of the money was flowing back into the state government. According to Reed, Clinton had "a secret ambition all along to be president. "He had a lot of work cut out for him. He had to build an industrial base and literally drag Arkansas up into the 20th century. The way he did that is through cooperation with the CIA, which we get into deeply in the book, about the money laundering projects and actually, government, certain industries, getting involved in the manufacturing of weapons components."

When Reed discovered that the Mena project included cocaine trafficking, he said, he pulled out of it, and that was when his troubles began.

Reed said he trained the Contra pilots at the request of Oliver North, whom he met in Oklahoma. At the time, he said, North was going by the code name "John Cathay.

"North and I hit it right off," Reed said in the radio interview. "And philosophically we agree." They both disliked former President Richard Nixon and his secretary of state, Henry Kissinger, Reed added.

North allegedly told Reed to donate a Piper aircraft Reed owned to the Contra cause, then to report the plane had been stolen and collect the insurance money.

Reed collected a $33,000 insurance payment, for the plane. According to an April 20, 1992, *Time Magazine* article, Thomas Baker, a Little Rock private investigator, found a rusted Piper in an Arkansas hangar. "He asked his best friend, Raymond "Buddy" Young, who had been President Clinton's chief of security for a decade, to run the plane's identification number through the FBI's national crime data base."

The plane turned out to be Reed's, according to the article.

Reed and his wife, Janis, were charged with insurance fraud in June 1988. Court documents show Reed said he needed Oliver North's diaries, notes, and phone records to be able to put on his case. When the federal government refused to turn them over, the judge presiding over the Reeds' case dismissed the charges.

Shortly afterward, the Reeds filed suit against Baker and Young, saying they had made a phony case against them.

Five years after Reed filed that lawsuit, a federal judge ruled Reed would not be permitted to introduce any evidence about his alleged connections to the CIA and FBI. The Reeds, who had already asked for numerous continuances, dropped their action at that point.

"Devastation does not come close to describing our feelings," Reed said in a statement issued shortly after the case was dismissed.

"After years of dragging this case through the federal civil justice system, Judge (George) Howard has manipulated us into the following legal posture. We can go to court, but we cannot put on critical evidence, therefore we will lose. That loss, even though we could appeal it, and the appeal would consume at minimum another year of our lives and tens of thousands of dollars, will be interpreted by Clinton spin doctors as a victory. There will be no mention of the fact that our hands were tied and our mouths were gagged and the so-called trial was a travesty of justice. They will attempt to convince the media at a critical point in the election process (the case was dismissed in May 1996 as Clinton was running for re-election) that Mena is a figment of my imagination, even though the Mena evidence was not allowed to be presented in court.

"Proudly being a former member of the U. S. armed services," Reed continued, "I was trained to win wars, not lose them. I refuse to repeat my Vietnam experience and not be allowed to win.

"With tears in our eyes, lumps in our throats and knots in our stomachs, we are instructing our attorney to non-suit this case."

Reed said, "I would like to think that my personal hero, Harry S Truman, would be proud of my accomplishments, even in the face of overwhelming odds. At times of strife, he was encouraged by the average citizen to 'Give 'em hell, Harry,' I, too, have heard voices who backed me shout, 'Give 'em hell, Terry.' "

Assistant Attorney General Rick Hogan, who told the Arkansas Democrat-Gazette Reed's lawsuit was only filed for its publicity value, was defending the Arkansas officials. "Nothing is going to stop this guy from writing books, going on talk shows, what have you. I don't think anything will silence these people, which I guess is one of the great things about this country."

Reed said the judge throwing out the evidence was part of a Clinton-based cover up. He never explained why a judge who had sentenced people in connection with the Whitewater scandal only a month earlier would be in on a conspiracy with the president.

*Time Magazine*, in that April 20, 1992, full-page article, entitled "Anatomy of a Smear," said that not only did Reed not have much evidence on Mena that would have made a difference in the case, but also that he was never involved in any CIA activities in the little Arkansas town.

"To hear Terry Reed tell it," *Time* writer Richard Behar began his article, "during the mid-1990s, he was a key player in a cover 'resupply network' that flew Nicaraguan Contras and drugs back to the U. S. using a small airport in rural Arkansas as a base.

"On top of that, the enterprise was personally supervised by Gov. Bill Clinton, whose state received 10 percent of the profits from the operation. And according to Reed, he even discussed the scheme with Clinton while the governor smoked marijuana in a van parked outside a busy Mexican restaurant in Little Rock."

After that beginning, Behar continued, "The only trouble with Reed's sensational tale is that not a word of it is true."

*Time* did not say that nothing was going on at Mena. The article just indicated there was no credible evidence that Terry Reed had any connection with it.

"There is absolutely no proof Reed ever worked with the CIA," the article said. "Oliver North denies that he ever met or has spoken with him. A couple with whom Reed claims he was dining on the night of his alleged conversation with Clinton says they have never been to the restaurant with Reed."

The article continued to delve into Reed's background, saying that prior to 1992 he spent a number of years jumping from one job to another "leaving behind a string of charges that he absconded with company funds. Among his victims: an Illinois-based Japanese machine tool company named Gomiya, which currently has a $600,000 judgment against him. Last month, U. S. marshals seized Reed's van for Gomiya."

Reed blamed his problems on the CIA, according to the *Time* article. He eventually filed a libel suit against the magazine. "Back when I was young and naïve," he said during the 1994 radio interview.

The case was thrown out of court. Reed said, "It was dismissed by a federal judge. We just didn't have the resources to properly litigate it. They hit us with their gold-plated law firm and we just were ill equipped to throw the million dollars we needed into it.

"We felt *Time Magazine* had used all of their resources to protect Bill Clinton. When he wrote that article, Strobe Talbott (a former college roommate of the president) was a so-called editor-at-large for *Time Magazine*. My lawyers felt and I still feel that Strobe Talbott enlisted the services of *Time* and its staff to protect Bill in 1992, at a time in which the Mena scandal would have run back-to-back with the Gennifer Flowers scandal and probably kept him out of the White House.

"That symbol of justice, the blind lady with the scales," Reed continued, "she weighs justice; she weighs money. It's sad, but that's what the courts in this country have turned into. The O. J. Simpson case is a good example of that."

At that point in the radio interview, Reed mentioned the lawsuit he had dismissed against Baker and Young. "We saw that Judge Howard's intention was to get us (Reed and his wife) to pay for our own crucifixion. We're up against a powerful, powerful political machine that's obviously absorbed at least some federal judges and they're using those judges to protect politicians to keep the truth from coming out."

Reed said he planned to sue that judge and that he was "exploring his options." He talked about an appearance he had scheduled at the Mid-America Constitution Conference in Kansas City.

As I researched that conference, I noted the name of the president of the conference- Ann Funk, the same supposedly ordinary citizen and attendee of the American Heritage Festival who had joined the Reeds to sue *The Press* and me for $1.5 billion.

But Reed was not always the one who did the suing.

Arkansas businessman J. D. Brotherton, whose company, Brodix Manufacturing, was accused in Reed's book of making gun parts for the Contras, sued Reed for libel, I discovered as I continued my research.

Reed's book indicated Brotherton's company had been involved in "the secret, illegal manufacture of untraceable weapons," which was in violation of a Congressional ban on military aid to the Contras. Brotherton said Reed's book left the impression his company was being directed by the CIA and that it was involved with illegal Contra training and money laundering.

The lawsuit, Reed said during a radio interview, was going to provide him with a golden opportunity to get on the public record the Mena evidence that had been tossed out during his lawsuit against Baker and Young.

After saying on a number of conservative radio talk shows that he could not wait for his day in court, Reed abruptly reached a settlement with Brotherton August 8, 1996.

Randel Miller, Reed's attorney, told the *Arkansas Democrat-Gazette* Brotherton and Reed agreed to a "non-financial settlement."

That settlement involved Reed signing an affidavit saying he never meant to indicate Brotherton or his company had been involved in illegal activities.

*The Washington Weekly*, a conservative electronic news magazine, which had normally been supportive of Reed, quoted a source, who was not named, as saying the settlement was reached because "the trial could have been embarrassing for Reed."

An article from the July 5 1998, *St. Louis Post-Dispatch* indicated Reed was planning to sell Red Oak II property to survivalists who were concerned about the effect of the Y2K bug. "Terry Reed- a man who says he's not a conspiracy theorist but is accustomed to being labeled one- regularly participates in 'patriotic conferences' throughout the country. A former CIA agent who lives in Carthage, Missouri, Reed is the author of a book called *Compromised, Clinton, Bush and the CIA*, which has become a best seller in survivalist circles. Turner (Candace Turner of Sarcoxie) is making a Y2K presentation at a conference Reed will hold in Carthage in two weeks. Other guests include a local realtor who will advise attendees interested in relocating to rural Missouri for the millennium."

My research gave me an idea of what Terry Reed's next move would be. Reed was a fixture on right-wing radio and in the magazines as well as on the Preparedness Expo circuit. I had a feeling the American Heritage Festival lawsuit was about to become a regular topic in those venues.

Reed was not the only one associated with the American Heritage Festival who had a checkered history.

*Called to Serve*, Bo Gritz' 1991 book, included his belief in numerous conspiracies, including a plot in the '70s to put Nelson Rockefeller in the White House, and the theory that Richard Nixon was behind the November 22, 1963, assassination of President John F. Kennedy.

The book included this passage:

"One person who couldn't remember where he was or what he was doing when was also the candidate who benefited distinctly and directly from this violence, Richard Milhous Nixon. He is the only person who actually testified, who could not remember where he was on the day John Kennedy was murdered. It was easily proved that he was in Dallas that same day after attending a meeting the day before at the Clint Murchison ranch with a number of men described earlier (people vaguely connected to the assassination), including J. Edgar Hoover. The sole newspaper article that noted his presence in Dallas mentioned that both he and actress Joan Crawford were staying at the Baker Hotel while attending a meeting of Pepsi Cola executives. The son of a top Pepsi Cola executive first brought this fact to public attention, and it was later revealed that the son of another Pepsi Cola executive had dinner in Dallas with Jack Ruby (the man who shot assassin Lee Harvey Oswald to death) the night before Kennedy was murdered.

"Joan Crawford would later become the close drinking of companion of columnist Dorothy Kilgallen, the only journalist to obtain a jailhouse interview with Jack Ruby. After completing the interview, Kilgallen told friends that she had information that would 'blow the JFK case sky high.' Before her story could appear in print, however, she was found dead in her New York apartment. The apartment had been ransacked and all of her records and notes were missing. Her death was termed a 'suicide.' "

You get the idea. Gritz' "revelations" about the Kennedy assassination also connected future President George H. W. Bush, and dozens of other top officials to the crime.

Another definite believer in shadowy conspiracies was Rep. Charles Key, who claimed the U. S. government was behind the Oklahoma City bombing. The Oklahoma Republican told *Washington Weekly* in its June 29, 1998 issue:

"I don't know that we have any new evidence on people's identities. But the evidence clearly points to other perpetrators and a bigger conspiracy to bomb the building than McVeigh and Nichols. There are many eyewitnesses to other perpetrators. Scientific experts say it could not have happened with an ammonium nitrate bomb. Other experts say there would have been clear evidence of an ammonium nitrate bomb. which obviously was not found at the site. There are people such as the person we just discussed, who talk about other explosive devices they saw taken out of the building, or say they talked to federal personnel about those devices being removed from the building after the initial explosions. So I think the evidence is overwhelming. You don't have a building there anymore so most evidence must come from witness reports."

With Dr. Leonard Horowitz, another Festival speaker, it was the idea that the CIA started the AIDS virus, which at that time, was spreading across the U. S. and the world.

In his book, *Emerging Viruses: AIDS and Ebola*, Dr. Horowitz wrote, "It has been theorized, and circumstantial evidence in this book supports the theory, that black Africans and American homosexuals may have been targeted for viral weapons experimentation by activities in America's military-medical-industrial complex and agents for the CIA.

"According to the Church Commission hearings, Henry Kissinger, and by association, Elmo Zumwalt or Melvin Laird, and Sidney Gottlieb ordered or administered the development and/or stockpiling of biological weapons, including immune system destroying viruses functionally identical to HIV, and the deployment of systems necessary to administer these viruses to large populations. Frank Carlucci, Joseph Califano, and Alexander Haig may also have been involved."

A week had passed since the lawsuit had been filed, so I walked up to Ralph Bush's office, and saw him hunched over his computer surfing the net, which was how he spent most of the day each day.

He looked up as I knocked on the open door. "Yes?"

"When are we supposed to meet with the lawyers?" I asked.

"I haven't heard anything," he said, and returned to surfing the internet.

I was being sued for three quarters of a billion dollars and I still had not heard one word from a lawyer representing The *Carthage Press'* interests.

As I write this, nearly 11 years later, I still have not talked with a *Carthage Press* lawyer about the case.

# MOVING FORWARD

As anyone who has ever been involved in a lawsuit knows, things move at a glacial pace. It's not like the TV legal shows where the action is brought at the beginning of the program, the trial takes place and the jury has rendered its verdict, all in the space of one hour.

If you are the defendant in a lawsuit, it hangs over your head for weeks, months, and many times years. And since I am one of those people who dwells on setbacks, the libel suit became the driving factor in my life.

When I was finished with my work for the day, I got on one of the two newsroom computers that had internet access (talk about how times have changed) and researched, trying to find anything I could about Terry Reed or the American Heritage Festival.

In the back of my mind, I knew what I was doing was not going to help my case, but I had to do something. Otherwise, I would have felt helpless.

If the libel suit had not been filed, this might have been the best time of my years at *The Carthage Press*. After a summer of working shorthanded, I finally convinced Ralph Bush to loosen the purse strings. We had already brought in former *Joplin Globe* reporter Jo Ellis, who had taken over coverage of our city government, county government, and police and sheriff's department beats.

I also convinced Ralph to hire another general assignment reporter and a sports editor. After going through dozens of less than qualified applicants, I contacted two former Missouri Southern State College students who had worked for me in

1995 and who had gone on to work on a Baxter Springs, Kansas, paper which had just gone out of business.

John Hacker had served a brief time as sports editor of *The Press*, driving over from the college to work the night shift. Writing sports was not John's strong suit, but he performed admirably in the role. John was and is a reporter's reporter. He is one of those who cannot rest if there is one more person to call for a story or one more story left to cover.

John's sense of curiosity was his greatest strength. He always wanted to know why things happened, and more often than not, he was able to find out. People trusted John and were often surprised by how much they revealed to him.

John was older than the normal recent college graduate. He was already in his 30s when he returned to *The Press*.

The new sports editor, Rick Rogers, had worked as a stringer for John, covering area sporting events when John was sports editor.   At MSSC, he was renowned as a design wizard. With John and Rick, we were adding two versatile reporters who would improve not only the content, but also the look of *The Press*.

With Jo, John, Rick, Ron Graber, and me as full-time news department employees, and the recent high schooler Jana Blankenship continuing to work part-time, we had the strongest staff in my five years at the helm.

John and Rick joined the staff in mid-August and after that, though the lawsuit was moving slowly, changes at *The Carthage Press* were not.

Though we subscribed to the Associated Press, our front pages were 100 percent local, and often we had so many local stories, we either had to move some inside or save them for the next day.

Jo was providing us with blanket coverage of city government, relying on her talent, strong work ethic, and more than two decades of experience at the *Globe*.

With John Hacker, we were able to cover news stories that might have slipped through the cracks in the past. When a Lamar, Missouri soldier, Staff Sgt. Kenneth Hobson, died during a terrorist bombing at the United States embassy in Kenya, John and Ron Graber gave *The Press* the best coverage, bar none, of any media outlet that covered the story.

When a big story hit our reading area, we threw everything at it. One such instance was the death of one of the best-known people in southwest Missouri, former Seventh District Congressman Gene Taylor.

John and Ron covered the Congressman's funeral, while I was able to provide background stories, and rerun a five-part series I had written earlier in which I had interviewed Rep. Taylor about the five presidents with whom he had worked during his 16 years in Congress.

And it wasn't just stories like that. With the staff we had, we were able to offer more sweeping coverage of the everyday news stories that are the bread and butter of a small-town daily newspaper.

Every event in the annual week long Carthage Maple Leaf Festival was covered with the same thoroughness.

And it was during that week that we introduced a major new design, courtesy of Rick Rogers and Ron Graber. I would love to say that the new crisp, clean, vibrant look to *The Carthage Press* was my brainchild, but the truth was, other than giving the go-ahead for it, and approving it when it was done, I had absolutely nothing to do with the redesign.

I was an editor/reporter, a guarantee I received from Jim Farley when he first appointed me managing editor in 1993.
I knew the only way I could put out the kind of newspaper I wanted was to have Randy Turner as a reporter. If I had confined my duties to editing and managing the newsroom budget, I would have lost a general assignment reporter, a sports reporter, an investigative reporter, a columnist, and a sports columnist, as well as a serviceable photographer.

When I became editor, I took on more duties, but not the traditional duties performed by most daily newspaper editors, especially in the Liberty Group Publishing chain. I did not paginate (constructing the pages on computer). I did not stay in the newsroom all day long to deal with whomever had a problem with the newspaper, and I did not participate in long, boring meetings to determine the newsroom budget.

I directed our coverage of news in Carthage and the surrounding area, worked up a page one dummy each morning for Ron to paginate, and worked as a writing and reporting coach.

And now with four strong reporters working with me, I was looking forward to being part of a newsroom Shangri-La.

We began promoting the new news team with an ad that ran in the September 10, 1998 *Press*. The *Press* banner was at the top; immediately under it was the slogan- "Big Time Coverage, Small Town Appeal."

Our ad salesman Stewart Johnson, who was also an award-winning photographer, took a picture of us across the street from the *Press* building outside of the Methodist Church. While Jana Blankenship and Jo Ellis sat on a concrete bench, the smiling foursome of John Hacker, Rick Rogers, Ron Graber, and me stood behind them.

Underneath the photo caption, the ad continued, "*The Carthage Press* has an experienced news staff dedicated to providing the most complete coverage of Carthage offered by any area media outlet.

"*Press* reporters have more than half a century of experience in covering the Carthage area and have earned more than 125 journalism awards in the past decade.

"For the best coverage of Carthage available anywhere, read *The Carthage Press*."

There was a new energy at *The Press* and people around Carthage were quick to pick up on it.

Unfortunately, in the back of my mind during all of this time, often moving to the front when I had time to think about it was the American Heritage Festival lawsuit.

The September 21, 1998 *Press* featured two articles about the festival. The first, filed by Associated Press, revealed that Festival speaker Bo Gritz had been hospitalized after shooting himself. The second involved some national publicity being given to Terry Reed's "patriotic Woodstock."

The festival was featured in the September 1998 issue of the far right magazine, *Media Bypass*, in a four-page article entitled, "Patriots Go Mainstream with 'Heritage Festival.'" Compared to the Terry Reed lawsuit that claimed the event was a failure and potential investors in Red Oak II (or Red Oak III) had been run off because of me, the rest of the media, and Jasper County elected officials, this article made it appear that the festival was the event of the century.

The article opened, "Three days, 70 vendors, spectacular speakers and thousands of visitors combined to make the first-ever American Heritage Festival a rousing success in this little corner of God's country."

According to the article, written by Gerald A. Carroll, the festival provided all of the information on "virtually every subject paramount in the minds of American patriots."

Those subjects, Carroll wrote, were "government-sanctioned drug trafficking, Gulf War Syndrome, the Y2K computer bug and suppression of musicians who happen to be politically incorrect." I had missed that last one somewhere along the line.

The article said that the event attracted a diverse crowd, though that diversity appeared to be referring to the presence of women.

The article featured quotes from some of the speakers, including those addressing the Oklahoma City bombing. " 'What appears clear to me is that at least two Iraqis were involved in the bombing,' (Hoppy) Heidelberg told the Precious

Moments audience. 'Timothy McVeigh and Terry Nichols might have had some involvement, but we are not being told of the true record of how many people executed this horrendous act against the people of Oklahoma and this nation.

Another speaker, Benton Partin, laid the blame for the Oklahoma City bombing on the federal government. "McVeigh was involved, but there is nothing to dissuade me from believing that his role started as a member of a counterterrorism unit sponsored by our own government. As the operation proceeded, he became so compromised that he simply took on the role as primary instigator and is willing to give up his own life while playing out that role."

The most fascinating descriptions from the *Media Bypass* article were of the presentation of Bo Gritz, the man whose burning of the United Nations flag and its depiction on page one of the Sunday *Kansas City Star* had captured the attention of people throughout the state of Missouri.

"Who is this anal orifice?" the article quotes Gritz as saying in a reference to Jasper County Sheriff Bill Pierce. "I understand that this sheriff told everyone that having the ROTC and the National Guard here would be a mockery of the flag because we're a bunch of hate-mongers. Well, that kind of New World Order attitude is on the way out."

The article included several paragraphs about Terry Reed, mentioning his book and his new video that explained how America was losing jobs to Mexico.

Following a rundown on the other speakers at the festival, Carroll's article turned to those who were not enthralled with the event.

*The Carthage Press* was not mentioned in the article, nor was I, but Carroll wrote, "There were some detractors. The *Kansas City Star*, known derogatorily as the Kansas City 'Red' Star in these parts, showed up, and reporter Judy Thomas did a decent job of getting most relevant facts in. However, she snooped a little too long at the literature tables and mentioned in her July 19 Sunday piece in the *Star* that the controversial novel, *The Turner Diaries*, was for sale at one of the tables. However, a scouring look revealed no copies of *The Turner Diaries* and very few openly racist books of any type.

"Of course, the alert editors at the *Star* just had to phone Mike Reynolds of the Southern Poverty Law Center whose 'watchdog' organization Klanwatch continuously prowls around the country, looking for such 'gatherings' to complain about.

Carroll quoted what Reynolds said about the festival, and then concluded his article by writing, "It was obvious the SPLC was caught off-guard and that Reynolds hilariously misrepresented the crowd in attendance. Give it up, Mike. You might as well bring your pal Morris Dees (head of the Southern Poverty Law Center to this day) for next year's festival and join them, belly up to the bar at the Red Oak II tavern. You'll be glad you did."

◆          ◆          ◆

As the weeks passed, I still had not heard anything from Liberty Group Publishing's lawyer. How could we be sued for $1.5 billion and not even consult with an attorney?

My first discussion with a lawyer came a few weeks after the lawsuit was filed, when Bernard Rhodes, with the Kansas City firm of Lathrop & Gage, called. When he told me, he was working as a lawyer for all of the media companies that were being sued, I felt comforted. Lathrop & Gage was probably the most powerful and well-known law firm in Missouri and having this guy on my side made me feel better.

He gave me a quick rundown of what was happening in the case, which at that point was not much, and he told me he would be back in touch.

A few days later, I received a large package by UPS that contained documents Rhodes had filed in federal court in an attempt to get the lawsuit dismissed.

The material was powerful and did not put the participants in the American Heritage Festival in a good light.

In the documents, which were filed October 6, 1998, Rhodes said that everything that had been written about the American Heritage Festival was true or it was constitutionally protected opinion.

Being the author of the best selling book, *Compromised: Clinton, Bush, and the CIA*, made Reed a public figure, Rhodes said, which increased his burden of proof. According to the 1964 *Sullivan vs. New York Times* case, actual malice had to be proved in libel suits against public figures. Rhodes noted that Reed said he had sold 250,000 hardcover and 500,000 paperback copies of the book. A 1994 listing on the *Los Angeles Times* best seller list for *Compromised* was included among the court filings.

"Reed has been the subject of more than 100 newspaper, magazine and wire service reports and editorials," the court documents said, including articles in *The Nation*, *The Wall Street Journal*, *The Washington Post*, *Arizona Republic*, *Arkansas Democrat-Gazette*, *Austin American-Statesman*, *The Dallas Morning News*, *Memphis Commercial Appeal*, *Minneapolis Star-Tribune*, and *St. Louis Post-Dispatch*.

"A Dec. 4, 1994, nationally televised report on Cable News Network (CNN) concluded 'the book written by Terry Reed (is) either not true, or at worst based on half-truths,' " the documents said.

"In its April 30, 1992, edition, *Time Magazine* published a full-page story on Terry Reed entitled "Anatomy of a Smear." Rhodes quoted the first paragraph of the *Time* story, which said everything Terry Reed wrote was false. "The article goes on to retell Reed's story about then-Governor Bill Clinton and alleged illegal drug smuggling and concludes, 'the only trouble with Reed's sensational tale is that not a word of it is true.' "

The documents also covered Reed's lawsuits against *Time Magazine* and Arkansas state officials. Those legal actions, as well as his numerous speaking engagements at the Preparedness Expo series of conventions, have kept him in the public limelight, the court documents said.

The documents also included the final ruling by Judge Whitman Knapp, U. S. District Court, Southern District of New York, in the libel suit filed by Reed against *Time Magazine* following writer Richard Behar's "Anatomy of a Smear" story.

In the ruling, dated January 6, 1995, Knapp wrote, "It cannot be disputed that Behar made a thorough examination of the story plaintiff had submitted to *Time Magazine*, Plaintiff had been unable to come up with any evidence suggesting that Behar did not in good faith believe that every fact stated in his article was accurate, and that his characterization of plaintiff as a liar was fully justified. The question of whether or not any or all of Behar's conclusions may have been mistaken is not before us."

"Advertisements for the Preparedness Expo conventions regularly appear in nationally circulated magazines and often feature Reed's picture and a short biography," the court documents said.

"Reed also spoke at 'Jubilation '96,' an annual convention sponsored by *The Jubilee*, a major Christian Identity newspaper. Other speakers at Jubilation '96 included Ku Klux Klan leader Louis Beam and Christian Identity leader Rev. Peter R. Peters." In an advertisement for sales from videos of that event, which was submitted as an exhibit, Reed's talks about the Mena coverup were sold along with videotapes by Beam, Peters, and Randy Weaver of Ruby Ridge fame.

In the court filing, Rhodes included an Inter-Klan Newsletter with the comment "Death to Every Foe and Traitor" at the top, with the byline of Louis Beam. Beam writes, "For every Aryan school of thought, the Jew has concocted a dark and insidious counterpart. And he has spent these long years easing his sick, Talmudic ideas into places once occupied by healthy Aryan ones."

Rev. Pete Peters, who also spoke at various expos with Reed, claimed God was a racist who preferred the white race, and that homosexuals should be given the death penalty.

The advertisement for Jubilee Videos from Jubilation '96 started with three names, Louis Beam, Pete Peters, and Terry Reed.

"Reed is a frequent guest on talk shows, often promoting his book," the document said. "(He) also operates "U. S. Awareness," which produces social-oriented documentaries based on current events that tear at the core of the American dream," the documents said, quoting the way Reed characterized the company.

"At the time of the American Heritage Festival, U. S. Awareness, was also 'currently spearheading an alternative community real estate development whose theme is self-sufficiency." In Reed's lawsuit, he claims the smear campaign against him prevented him from entering into a business agreement to operate Red Oak II and to develop Red Oak III."

*The Star's* attorneys also rebutted each item Reed claimed defamed him in their articles and columns. Reed said he was libeled by a quote from the July 19, 1998, *Kansas City Star* article in which Michael Reynolds of the Southern Poverty Law Center says, "You have at this event the conspiracies, you have Christian Identity, you have the speakers that are all the center of what is driving the Christian Patriot movement in the country. What this shows is that the white Christian separatists have become well-established in rural southwest Missouri."

"First of all," the lawyer argued, "he says absolutely nothing about Terry Reed. Rather, Reynolds' comment appears aimed generally at either the hundreds of thousands of people who live in rural southwest Missouri, the 1,500 to 3,000 people who attended the festival, or perhaps, the more than a dozen speakers who spoke at the festival or maybe even the more than 50 exhibitors who hawked their wares to festival-goers."

In addition to characterizing Reynolds' quotes as opinion, the *Star's* attorney noted that his statements were true. When he said there were conspiracies represented, the court document said, "Perhaps the best example of this fact is Reed himself, who has apparently made a living off a 670-page book that alleges a great conspiracy between then-Vice President Bush, then-Governor Bill Clinton, the CIA, and the Contras to import and sell illegal drugs in the United States. Other speakers at the festival echoed the conspiracy call, as did numerous exhibitors who fueled the conspiracy fire with their books and tapes."

Reynolds' statement that the Christian Identity movement was at the festival was true, if only because of its star attraction, Col. James "Bo" Gritz, the attorney said, as well as numerous exhibitors who featured Christian Identity material. "And one exhibitor even sold books urging readers to choose sides in the upcoming war against the Jews in order to reclaim "God's true Israel."

Reed also claimed he was defamed by *The Star's* mention that *The Turner Diaries*, which was described as a racist book, was being sold by one of the exhibitors. "Again, the fact that a certain book was for sale at the festival does not, in any way, defame Terry Reed. The article does not say Reed himself sold the book, nor does it say that Reed even knew the book was for sale."

The description of the book as racist is constitutionally-protected opinion, the *Star* attorney said, but noted that on the book's cover it says, "This Book Contains Racist Propaganda. The FBI said it was the blueprint for the Oklahoma City Bombing." The opening statement from the trial of convicted Oklahoma City bomber Timothy McVeigh, in which federal prosecutors make that claim, was included in Rhodes' court filing.

One exhibit included in the court filing contained pages from *The Turner Diaries*, including the following paragraph:

'The first thing I saw in the moonlight was the placard with its legend in large, block letters: 'I defiled my race.' Above the placard leered the horribly bloated, purplish face of a young woman, her eyes wide open and bulging, her mouth agape. Finally, I could make out the thin, vertical line of rope disappearing into the branches above...There are many thousands of hanging female corpses tonight, all wearing identical placards around their necks. They are the white women who were married to or living with blacks, with Jews or with other non-white males."

The court documents included excerpts from the book, *Satan's Kids,"* the title of which refers to the Jewish people, which was on sale at the festival, plus a catalog, which was available at the festival, featuring a number of other books which defamed blacks, Jews, Hispanics, and others.

Reed also claimed he was libeled in a statement that said the Carthage Chamber of Commerce did not sponsor the American Heritage Festival.

The *Star* article said, "Advertisements for the festival implied that the city of Carthage and Precious Moments, the company known worldwide for its collectible figurines, were co-sponsors of the event. Friday, however, the Carthage Chamber's executive director, Heather Kelly, said that wasn't true. 'We've done what we can to accommodate them. But we are not sponsoring it.' "

Advertisements for the festival were submitted in the court documents, including one that read, "Red Oak II, Precious Moments and the Historic Town of Carthage, Missouri, proudly invite you to rekindle your American spirit.

"Additionally, those same advertisements refer to Red Oak II, Precious Moments and the Historic Town of Carthage, Missouri, as the 'co-hosts of this must-attend event.' The court documents also included affidavits from Ms. Kelly, Carthage Mayor Kenneth Johnson and Precious Moments

Vice President James Malcolm saying the Chamber, city, and Precious Moments did not sponsor the festival.

The *Star* attorney concluded, "Terry Reed may not like what the *Kansas City Star* wrote about the American Heritage Festival '98. That does not, however, make the statements actionable."

Rhodes asked the court to dismiss the case against Judy Thomas and the *Kansas City Star* "and allow them to continue their work as independent watchdogs of the community, whether Terry Reed likes it or not."

Though neither *The Carthage Press* nor I was mentioned in Rhodes' voluminous filing, it still made me feel good that someone was going on the attack against Reed.

Over the next few weeks, I had a number of conversations with Rhodes, and after each one I felt better about the lawsuit. I was getting to the point where I was finally enjoying life a little bit again, and for me at that point in my life- everything was about my job.

Each day, I helped steer the content of the paper in the mornings, worked on stories during the afternoons, covered either meetings or ballgames at night, returned to the *Press* office and wrote my stories before signing off for another evening.

From 7:30 a.m. to approximately 1 a.m. the next day, my life belonged to *The Carthage Press*. It was not a healthy way of living, but at that point my whole self-worth was wrapped around my job. It was the only life I had.

Finally, one morning a letter arrived, the service for the American Heritage Festival lawsuit. I was not familiar with this way of serving people. My only acquaintance with someone being served came from television and movies. I did not know these things were done via the mail. Coincidentally, I received a call from Bernie Rhodes, a few moments after I received the letter.

"Randy, I don't know if you have heard, but I am not going to be representing you or *The Carthage Press*."

"What happened?'

"I'm not sure. Liberty Group Publishing indicated they were not interested in our services."

While I had him on the phone, I decided to ask him about the letter, and he patiently explained what my options were. "You can sign it and return it, or you can let them serve you."

"What happens if they serve me?"

"You would have to pay probably about $200. But don't worry about that, Randy. Whoever Liberty hires as your lawyer will take care of that for you. All you have to do is sit back and let the lawyers do their jobs."

He wished me luck. When we ended the conversation, I did not realize it was the last time I would ever talk to a lawyer about the libel suit.

After that, I was totally in the dark.

# ALL THE WAY TO THE WHITE HOUSE

As he had done with his previous lawsuits, Terry Reed began working the far-right media to drum up publicity in the weeks after he filed his petition.

*Media Bypass*, a bible for conspiracy theorists, printed a full-page article on the American Heritage Festival lawsuit in its October 1998 issue.

Though only one month had passed since the magazine had termed the American Heritage Festival "a rousing success," by this time the editors had fallen into line with Terry Reed and were upset with how the *Kansas City Star*, KMBZ, Randy Turner, *The Carthage Press*, Rep. Mark Elliott, and Jasper County elected officials had conspired to destroy the festival and to denigrate anyone who stepped foot on the grounds at Red Oak II or the Precious Moments Convention Center.

Reed was encouraging anyone who felt offended by the way the media and Jasper County officials handled the festival to join in the class action.

In the article, Reed claimed the defendants in the case were involved in a conspiracy against him:

*"'It was premeditated and planned,' said Reed, author of the famous George Bush-Bill Clinton expose' Compromised,*
*which blew the lid off the Arkansas-Central America drug trafficking connections during the 1980s. 'There is no getting around it. We had to go to court with this as much as I regret having to do so.'"*

Reed continued, "Some people who attended have suffered tremendously from the smear campaign. They have been labeled neo-Nazis, kooks, antigovernment crazies, gun fanatics, and racists. It isn't fair and we're doing something about it.

"If you attended and genuinely feel damaged by this smear campaign, you can become a party to this suit." He gave a website where the complaint could be found, ways that he could be contacted, and the article included the phone number of Reed's attorney, Todd Nielsen.

Even though I still had not talked to any lawyer for Liberty Group Publishing, *Kansas City Star* attorney Bernard Rhodes was kind enough to keep sending me copies of court filings. In one such filing, I found that Terry Reed had claimed the American Heritage Festival lawsuit could lead to the White House.

The statement was made during a July 30, 1998, radio interview on KCXL-AM, Liberty, Missouri, and WWCR (shortwave), in which Reed attempted to solicit more people to join in on the class action.

Rhodes filed a partial transcript of that program with the court. According to the transcript, Reed said, "If your neighbors have ridiculed you, if you've had any kind of threatening phone call or if you personally feel depressed as a result of having been here and feel that this is something you don't want to take, you don't want, you're not necessarily proud of or something that you don't really want to be discussing with friends, that you came to the American Heritage Festival, you feel slandered or ridiculed, we want to hear from you.

"We want to add you to the class action suit against the *Kansas City Star*, so please contact us and you can do that through the 800 number."

Reed, who was appearing on a program with American Heritage Festival speaker and former Populist Party vice presidential candidate Bo Gritz, said, "Bo, I only have about

600 names and addresses that I know were here and those were the people who paid by credit card. The rest who paid by cash, I have no way to knowing who came so it's really important we network and find the people that feel they have been slammed by the liberal press."

It was at that point, according to the transcript, that Reed says the information from the lawsuit could lead straight to the top. "The discovery element of this case could be really interesting," he said. "It could lead us into law enforcement files, it could lead into computerized databases being controlled by The White House to disrupt these kinds of events which are, of course, what they don't want to have happening, a peaceful gathering of concerned citizens. And that's what this was."

Later, Reed mentioned the portion of the lawsuit that was directed against the Jasper County Sheriff's Department. "What's ironic about this," Reed said, "this is what the festival was about. Was about a government out of control. And they came down here and prove to us how out of control they actually are.

"Like Todd Nielsen (Reed's attorney and another festival speaker) said, very seldom do you find a sheriff this stupid, to openly go out and disseminate this kind of data. But he did so. He had his deputies out doing it. They did everything in their power to disrupt us. I feel like I'm in good old Mother Russia and this is the KGB."

Among the documents filed October 6, 1998, was a request for the judge to quickly dismiss the lawsuit. "Quick action in this case is vital because of the threat that it poses to the First Amendment." Quoting from the 1966 case of Washington Post Co. vs. Keogh, the document said, "In the First Amendment area, summary procedures are essential. For the stake here, if harassment succeeds, is free debate."

Rhodes wrote, "Here, Terry Reed has a track record of filing frivolous defamation claims, using the discovery process for the ulterior purpose of influencing public opinion and then dismissing those claims after having them pend for years. And in a preview of a repeat performance, Reed has publicly suggested, in soliciting support for his current lawsuit against *The Star*, that he intends to use (it) for much the same purpose.

"As such, it is vitally important that this court take an early critical examination of Reed's lawsuit to ensure that the mere pendency of this lawsuit does not, in itself, trample upon the First Amendment."

About the time these documents were sent to me, the deadline arrived to decide whether or not to sign and return the papers I had been sent through the mail.

Since Bernard Rhodes had told me that not returning them would cost us about $200 if we had to be served in person, and since I was not the one who was in charge of my defense, I took the papers into Ralph Bush's office.

I asked if I should send the papers back and what our lawyers had said.

"I haven't talked to any lawyers yet," Ralph said. I didn't say anything, but I had a hard time understanding why his newspaper was being sued for $1.5 billion and he had not insisted upon talking to an attorney.

I explained the options as Rhodes had explained them to me. When I was finished, Ralph hesitated for a moment, and then said, "We don't want to spend $200, so you might as well go ahead and send them in."

I signed the papers and put them in the box to go out with the mail. Though I did not know it at the time, those signatures ended up costing me my job.

# NUMBER FIVE IN
# THE STATE

As anyone who has ever been through a lawsuit knows, weeks can pass with nothing happening. During this time, I was having no problem getting used to having perhaps the strongest staff of any small daily newspaper in the state.

We introduced our redesign in an October 1998 edition that had a story and color photo of newly crowned Carthage Maple Leaf Queen Kacey Baugh at the top of page one, and a story about the *Kansas City Star* mounting an aggressive defense against the Terry Reed lawsuit at the bottom.

On Oct. 31, 1998, some good news actually came our way. On that day, *The Carthage Press*, published in a community of just 11,000 people and with a staff of only five, captured fifth place in the Missouri Press Association Better Newspaper Gold Cup competition all from entries that took place long before we had beefed up our staff with Jo Ellis, John Hacker, and Rick Rogers. This gave me high hopes for what *The Press* could do in the future.

We captured 10 MPA awards to finish behind only the Gold Cup winner that year (and nearly every year) the *Kansas City Star*, the *St. Louis Post-Dispatch*, the *Springfield News-Leader*, and the *Columbia Daily Tribune,* the four biggest newspapers in the state.

We had three first place awards. Ron Graber took the title in Spot News Photo for a picture of a couple watching as their house burned. Our former sports editor Brian Webster, branching out from sports, won first in feature writing for his story on a reunion at the Springfield/Branson Regional Airport of a Lamar family with its relatives from Kosovo.

I was proud of Ron and Brian for their accomplishments, but the big-ticket award as far as I was concerned was our first place in Community Service for Teen Tuesday, a regular page in our Tuesday edition that we devoted to teen news, with teens providing all of the stories and photos.

The idea for Teen Tuesday was mine, but the success of the project was primarily due to a Carthage High School senior named Stacy Rector, who by this time was a freshman at the University of Missouri at Columbia.

Stacy was a multi-talented young woman, who was equally adept at writing features and hard news. Her Teen Tuesday pages not only covered the typical information about what was going on at the school, but she also delved deeply into issues that affected teens.

And Stacy was there to accept the first place plaque. Also there was Brooke Pyle's younger brother, Matthew, who had also been a key contributor to Teen Tuesday, providing photos and doing darkroom work.

Stacy was not the only college student to take home an award that day for *The Press*. Cait Purinton, a Kansas State University student, who had worked for the newspaper during the summers of 1996 and 1997, was only 19 when she wrote the investigative series that took third place in the Best Investigative Reporting category and fourth place for best coverage of government.

Her series on problems at the Guest House, a Lamar residential care facility, detailed the financial problems of its owners, and used documents to explain how an arson fire, a savage beating, and other incidents led to the state of Missouri's decision to close the facility.

Cait discovered information on the firm's bankruptcy, its owing federal and state taxes, and other things that had not been uncovered by the state agency in charge of residential care facilities.

Our five other awards included the following:

— Ron Graber took second place, losing only to our own Brian Webster in best feature story, for an exploration of juvenile offenders' visit to a state prison.
— Teen Tuesday helped us take fourth place for Best Coverage of Young People.
— Fourth place for Best Family Living Coverage
— Fourth place for Ron Graber in the Spot News Photo category
— Third place for Brian Webster in Best Feature Photo

One thing in which I always took pride was that the awards won by *The Carthage Press* were won for its coverage of everyday news in the community. Year after year, I have seen newspapers that excel at covering catastrophic events, like tornadoes or multiple murders and rack up awards by the dozens. At *The Press*, we collected our awards for covering the news 12 months, 52 weeks every year.

Our successes at that 1998 convention were captured on film by John Hacker, who shot the photo of MPA President Bill James of the *Cass County Democrat Missourian*, Cait Purinton, Stacy Rector, me, Matthew Pyle, Ron Graber, and Ralph Bush that ran across the top of page one of the November 2, 1998, *Carthage Press*.

Ironically, on a day when the *Kansas City Star* received the Gold Cup Award and *The Carthage Press* had finished fifth, another defendant in the American Heritage Festival lawsuit was being honored.

Rep. T. Mark Elliott received the first Missouri Press Association Sunshine Award for his efforts in making substantial changes to the state's Open Meetings Law.

◆     ◆     ◆

A couple of weeks after our triumphant day at the Missouri Press Association convention, Ralph Bush stuck his head into the newsroom shortly after that day's pages had been sent to Neosho to be printed and asked, "Randy, can you come into my office for a second?"

I did not like the tone of that question.

When we arrived at the office, he said, "Randy, you are in big trouble."

I did not respond.

"I got a call this morning. Ken Serota is extremely upset about your waiving the service for the lawsuit." At that time, Ken Serota, a lawyer, was CEO of Liberty Group Publishing.

"Why?"

"After you signed the papers and returned them," Ralph said, "you have to respond to the lawsuit in 30 days."

Bernie Rhodes, the *Kansas City Star's* lawyer, had never told me that, nor had I asked him. Ralph continued, "If you don't respond, the judge can issue a judgment against you."

"For $750 million?"

"For $750 million. But that is not going to happen. The judge figured something was not right about this, so he called Ken Serota and bawled him out for not consulting a lawyer about this libel suit. So he is mad about being embarrassed by the judge and he is mad because we are going to have to spend $10,000 for a lawyer."

"Why $10,000?"

"It will cost a lot more, but that is the deductible on our libel insurance."

My mind was reeling at this information. "So let me see if I understand. We were going to put off talking to a lawyer as long as we could to save money?"

Ralph did not say anything.

"And Ken Serota is mad, when I am the one who is being sued for $750 million for writing an opinion column?"

Ralph nodded. "That's why you shouldn't have signed those papers."

That's when the realization hit me. Ralph Bush had provided either Ken Serota or our regional manager a version of what happened that didn't jibe with reality.

"I asked you if I should sign them," I reminded him.

Ralph looked down. "That's not how I remember it."

I asked if there was anything else. Ralph said there wasn't, so I returned to the newsroom.

"What's up?" Ron Graber asked.

"I've been hung out to dry."

From that moment on, I knew that if anything went wrong with the American Heritage Festival lawsuit, my job was on the line. In the back of my mind, I wondered if my days at *The Carthage Press* were numbered.

# *ABANDONED*

I had sort of a schizophrenic existence at *The Press* for the next few months.

I went back and forth between worrying about the American Heritage Festival lawsuit and enjoying the day-to-day successes of our news team.

The top moments journalistically came in December 1998 when we ran a weeklong series tackling the problem of drunk driving.

We started it on the day after Christmas, traditionally a time when newspapers started running retrospectives of what happened during the previous year. In the Saturday, December 26, 1998, *Press* we opened the series with Jo Ellis' story about a Carthage family which had been devastated when a drunk driver killed the mother, my article, taken from court documents, about judges restoring driving privileges to drunk drivers, and a rare page one editorial describing the series.

On Monday, December 28, Jo had the lead story, a profile of Jasper County Circuit Court Judge Joseph Schoeberl, a man known for being tough on drunk drivers. I wrote about how special interests and lobbyists had derailed tough drunk driving laws in the Missouri Legislature.

The Tuesday, December 29, edition featured my story on a DWI case that led to a murder conviction, Jo's report on the Carthage Police Department's approach to curbing drunk driving, and Cait Purinton's description of how the Missouri Highway Patrol prepared for New Year's Eve.

On our opinion page that day, I wrote about a drunk driver who had been mollycoddled by the law for nearly four decades.

Wednesday, December 30's *Press* included my feature on the Phipps family of Lamar, which was devastated by a 1995 drunk driving accident in which a man who had a dozen DWI arrests, plowed into their car while going more than 100 miles per hour killing eight-year-old Julie Phipps and permanently injuring her father, Jerry Phipps, and younger sister Abby. John Hacker added a story about the efforts of Mothers Against Drunk Drivers.

The series concluded December 31, 1998, with Rick Rogers' feature on Scott Hettinger, a Carthage Senior High School coach who lost the use of his legs in a drunk driving accident, Jo's feature on how top local Mothers Against Drunk Driving officials had become involved with the organization, and my page one column saying it was time for all of us to get involved in the battle against drunk driving.

I had never been prouder of a news staff. It was a powerful, well-received series.

But in the midst of that triumph and others from the powerhouse staff we had put together, I no longer felt I had much of a future at the newspaper.

I felt like a ghost walking through the *Carthage Press* building. I kept waiting for the ax to fall, but something worse happened, ironically, on April Fool's Day 1999.

I received a letter, sent to my home address, from Media/Professional Insurance, the company that was now handling the libel suit.

In bold caps at the top of the page it said "IMMEDIATE RESPONSE REQUIRED" and "SECOND REQUEST." I did not remember having ever seen a first request.

It included the following paragraph:

> *Enclosed is a statement in the amount of $7,855.84, which our office received for services rendered in connection with the referenced claim. A deduction has been taken from the attached statement, and this statement also reflects a past due amount that was*

*payable under the deductible or retention. If the previous*
*bill has not been paid, you should issue payment in the*
*amount of $7,798.76.*

This could not be happening. Why wasn't *The Carthage Press* handling this bill? I didn't have $7,798.76 in my bank account. I had about $500 in checking and a little over $1,000 in savings. I was making about $500 a week.

When I asked Ralph if I was going to have to pay the bill, he shrugged his shoulders and said, "I don't know. I'll see what I can find out."

It was the last I ever heard from Ralph on the subject. However, I never received another bill from the law firm and since it has been 10 years since the lawsuit ended, if I still owe it money, the interest is going to be huge.

# *THE BEGINNING*
# *OF THE END*

Having an envelope from your own boss marked "Confidential" sitting on your desk when you return from lunch is never a good thing and I hesitated before I opened it.

I already could sense that my time at *The Carthage Press* was coming to an end, and two times before, Ralph Bush's uncle, Richard Bush, had fired me by letter. Could it run in the family?

As I read the letter, I quickly realized I was not being fired. It did not take long for me to figure out that the groundwork was being laid for just that step.

This was the letter that was going to be put into my personnel file, outlining all of the problems I was creating for the newspaper.

Some of the things Ralph included in the letter were absolutely new to me. Some were blown way out of proportion and were not really problems.

> *Randy:*
>
> *I have several concerns that need to be addressed concerning your position as Managing Editor at the Carthage Press.*
>
> *I am receiving complaints regularly about events that take place in Carthage that we are not covering. One example is the recent MDA fundraiser. I specifically told you at the department head meeting that I wanted*

*to get something in the paper. To my knowledge, we did not run anything on it. We have a horrible track record for running business openings and ribbon cuttings. They either do not run at all or they run so long after the event that it is ridiculous. We ran a picture of a child with a fish caught on opening day of trout season weeks after the picture was taken and that was only after I came back twice and asked about it. It is YOUR responsibility to insure that these items run on a timely basis.*

*I have told you repeatedly that any overtime needs to be authorized by me in advance. Your department is consistently turning in overtime. Ron had over 15 hours of overtime on the last payroll. This was not approved in advance. We did pay the overtime because I assume he was working on assignments that you gave him. Your department is substantially over budget on payroll even without overtime. You need to adjust the workload so that it can be done without overtime. We are also going to have to make staff reductions to get back within budget on our payroll expense.*

*It would be great if we had local "hard news" stories every day-but we do not. We are taking stories and blowing them way out of proportion in an effort to make a story out of it. The recent Consumers disaster is a good example. The most recent story did not have anything in it except more speculation about the store closing. We have already run the same story several times without telling the readers anything new. The only thing new in the story was the information about the ad that was scheduled for the next week. There is enough happening that we do not need to make more out of a story than it deserves. If we are not telling the readers anything new-don't run the story.*

*If we have a significant national story, I want to see it on our front page. I do not want to force someone to go buy the Globe in order to find out what is going on in the world.*

*Our advertising department, as well as the other departments, works for the same paper as you do. I expect you to make every effort to work with them and help them. The editorial department will help with special projects. You will also need to work with advertising to insure that any news information that is provided by our advertisers gets into the paper on a timely basis.*

*I have had several complaints about being treated rudely or sarcastically by you. These complaints have come both from employees and from the public. I expect you to treat our staff and our readers courteously and with respect.*

*A significant part of your position is to insure that we do not publish things like the recent story on Consumers. When John wrote the story, you should have reviewed it BEFORE it went in the paper. YOU SHOULD BE READING THE FRONT PAGE BEFORE IT GOES OUT. Before we publish anything that might be controversial, I expect you to discuss it with me. This would include news and editorial.*

*You can consider this your notification that you are being placed on 90 day probation If you have any questions about any of these items I will be glad to discuss them, but these things listed here are not optional.*

*Ralph Bush*
*Publisher*

The axe was getting ready to swing. By this time, I had already begun removing my belongings. The row of wooden plaques I had won from the Missouri Press Association and Kansas City Press Club had long since been removed to my apartment. My desk was almost empty. I could not understand why this was happening…and Ralph Bush's letter was a laundry list of nonsense.

He had a legitimate complaint about Ron's overtime, but the rest of it was ridiculous, especially the part about my department being over budget. It had been Ralph's decision to pay the money to upgrade the news staff with the additions of Jo Ellis, John Hacker, and Rick Rogers.   And I had always worked with the advertising, circulation, and composing departments, and while we occasionally had differences, it was nothing like the war Ralph described in his letter.

And he was upset with me for having too much local news on page one? This was the first time I had ever heard of that being a problem and he had never mentioned anything about it before. When there was a major national or international story I put it on page one, but no one was buying *The Carthage Press* for national news. Besides, we were advertising our strong news staff and its extensive coverage of local news.

The child with the fish picture that Ralph mentioned ran within days, not weeks, after we received it, and I could not recall him mentioning it to me once, let alone twice, and we ran all of the ribbon cutting photos we had on a once a week basis.

And where in the world did he get off saying I had been rude to customers? That was something I prided myself on. Our readers may not always like the things I wrote, but I was always polite to those who came into the office, talked to me on the phone, or those I came across while covering news stories.

The Consumers business was undeniably a problem. I disagreed with Ralph on that, but he was the boss. John Hacker, through some diligent reporting, had discovered that Consumers which had announced its closing, but had not given a specific date, was placing the exact same ad in *The Press* that it had placed in another city right before it shut its doors for good.

It was not a story that John Hacker slipped past me and got onto page one. I approved the story and thought he did excellent work on it.

Consumers, naturally, was not happy with it since it cut business down for a time while customers waited for the final big sales.

But for Ralph to accuse me of not reading the front page before it went to print (and to do it in all capital letters, no less) was a cheap shot and totally inaccurate. I read every word that was on page one (and nearly every other page) every day. That was my job.

It was tempting to march right into Ralph's office and tell him to shove his job where the sun doesn't shine, and I did give the idea some consideration, but only briefly. Either I was going to ride this one out, or Ralph was going to fire me.

There was no way in hell I was going to make it easy for him.

I resolved to just keep doing my job. My job got a bit tougher when we ran an accident photo that accidentally showed the foot of a dead person.

I honestly did not see the foot, and no one else thought much of it on the news staff, but it started an uproar in the community, including phone calls and letters to the editor talking about how little decency I had and how little regard I had shown for the family. A few of the letter-writers said it was time for Ralph Bush to show me the door.

"Just give him time," I thought. "You will get your wish."

I did not think things could get worse, but they did Ralph called me into the office one morning and announced that he was going to fire John Hacker.

"John is the best reporter we have. Why would we want to fire him? Is this about the Consumers story?

" He showed poor judgment on that story."

"If he showed poor judgment on that story then I showed poor judgment on that story," I said. "I approved it."

"That doesn't matter. We have to let him go. I just wanted you to know before I do it." I had the feeling the decision had been made by someone much further up the food chain than Ralph Bush.

The best reporting team on any small town daily in Missouri was a thing of the past. Ralph fired John Hacker a few moments after our conversation.

My biggest regret is that I did not turn in my resignation at that point to show my support for John. Instead I stood by and did nothing.

And John was just the first to go. It wasn't long after John's firing that Rick Rogers informed me he was taking a job at Missouri Southern State College working in the communications department. Rick's impending departure surprised me since Rick and Ralph had become good buddies over the past several months.

I placed an advertisement for a sports editor and I had much better luck in finding one than I did during my spring 1998 search that only brought The Press Max Metsinger.

The top candidate came from the same Missouri Southern communications factory that had produced Rick Rogers and John Hacker. Andre Smith had done some stringer work for Rick, and was a gifted writer, as well as being skilled in layout. The transition would not be that difficult.

For the time being, I was not being allowed to replace John Hacker.

I knew there was a good chance I was heading into my last days at *The Carthage Press* and I intended to make the best of it.

My last few weeks at *The Carthage Press* featured some of my best work. As I had done every year since arriving at *The Carthage Press*, I interviewed each member of Carthage Senior High School's top 10 students and ran them in a 10-part series beginning early in May.

When old friend Melody Hedeman from nearby Lockwood got married in late April, I surprised her with a feature on the wedding, which turned into a well-received column.

One of my favorite stories was a celebration of the 30th anniversary of our composing room foreman Jennifer Martin's first day at *The Press*.

Jennifer had been rock solid during my entire nine and a half years at the newspaper, often offering me a sounding board during troubled times, and I had taken advantage of that sounding board during these troubled times.

Jennifer's story included the following passage:

> *The only person who has been at The Press nearly as long as Jennifer, advertising salesman Stewart Johnson, a 25-year veteran, says, "Jennifer's dedication it second to none."*
>
> *Her patience is also second to none, Stewart said. "It seems like just yesterday that she said to me for the first time, 'You ain't going to get that in, buddy. You're way past deadline.'"*
>
> *Fortunately for Stewart, the good-natured Jenny almost always relents and the late advertisements make their way into The Press.*

The article concluded this way:

> *Though the methods of putting out this newspaper have changed greatly in the last three decades, one constant has remained. For 30 years, Jennifer Martin's skill, dedication, and professionalism have played a key role in the success of The Carthage Press.*

Sadly, Jennifer's time at *The Press* did not last much longer than my own.

One story I did in April did not seem that special to me at the time, but ended up being so a few months later. I was familiar with Dr. Greg Smith from his days as an assistant superintendent in the Webb City schools and as superintendent at Sarcoxie. When he took a new position as superintendent of the Diamond R-4 School District, I wrote the story.

During my final few days I covered graduations at some of our area high schools. I did the Sarcoxie graduation Friday,

May 14, and then fittingly, chronicled the Lamar High School graduation the following evening.

My final issue at *The Carthage Press* was Monday, May 17, 1999. I had three stories in the paper, including the Lamar High School graduation coverage, and an opinion page column on the Carthage Chamber of Commerce's Leadership Carthage program.

I had finished doing the page one dummy for Ron, when Ralph called me into his office and fired me.

# THE NEW REGIME

For the next few days, I couldn't eat and I couldn't sleep. I had practically given my entire life to *The Carthage Press* for nearly a decade and now I had nothing.

It was a stupid way to think, but I really did not have anything in my life. I had been a 24-hour-a-day reporter/editor. Even on vacations, I never went anywhere. I often ended up covering stories, or doing research for projects I wanted to do when the vacation ended. I was always the one who worked the VFW's Memorial Day program at Park Cemetery, so the others could enjoy their holiday…and because I really did not have anything else to do.

What a pathetic way to spend my life, I thought, as I lied in bed and looked at the ceiling of my apartment. I began the job search almost immediately. On the first day, I compiled a list of newspaper addresses. I did not want to be unemployed. I had gone through that in the past and hated the helpless feeling, and the nagging doubt that anyone is ever going to hire you.

The day after I was fired, I filed for unemployment benefits. I was hoping I would never have to receive a check, but I had to get in my waiting week.

That night, I walked to a convenience store and picked up the first *Carthage Press* not to have Randy Turner as managing editor since December 1993.

I was stunned when I saw my replacements on page one. The new co-editors of the newspaper were Ron Graber (that did not surprise me, Ron had paid his dues and deserved a promotion) and Rick Rogers.

Wasn't Rick Rogers going to Missouri Southern?

The article said Rick was going to be in charge of news and sports and Ron would handle photos and features. That seemed to put the power in Rick's hands.

Had everyone been lying to me about this? Had Rick's ascension been planned all along, and was the Missouri Southern job just something to throw me off the trail?

I immediately put that thought out of my head. That was a ridiculous idea. Besides, I had heard people at Southern talking about it, so the MSSC job was real.

With so much time to think, I began to get more than a bit paranoid. Had Rick been greasing the skids for me during his social occasions with Ralph telling him what a horrible managing editor and evil person I was?

The person I was going to hire as sports editor, Andre Smith, got that job, but, of course, he was an old friend of Rick's from the college. When I interviewed Andre, did he already know Rick was going to be the man in charge? The more I thought about it, the more ludicrous that seemed.

As months went on, I kept hearing from people at The Press about how Rick talked constantly about how much better the newspaper was than it had been before, and in many ways it was.

Rick still had a strong staff, including Ron Graber, Jo Ellis, and two fresh new voices, Andre Smith and the returning Stacy Rector, who took over the lifestyle editor duties.

The paper was easily more attractive (my emphasis was always content), the photos were as sharp as ever, and the writing was uniformly good. Stacy was the best feature writer the newspaper had on its staff since Amy Lamb's departure in early 1998.

Other than meeting coverage, however, the hard news edge the newspaper had during my tenure vanished, as did all semblance of investigative reporting.

What had made *The Carthage Press* stand out for nearly a decade had changed, something that was likely to happen eventually anyway.

The new journalism, all packaging and no punch, was not something that I could have handled. If I had not been forced out in May 1999, I have no doubt looking back over 10 years that it would not have been long before this old war horse was put out to pasture.

# THIRD IN THE STATE
# AND NOBODY KNEW IT

My final farewell to 22 years as an editor and reporter was chronicled in the November 6, 1999, *Carthage Press*, nearly six months after I was fired.

On that day, during a luncheon in Columbia, *The Carthage Press* had its best showing ever in the Missouri Press Association's Better Newspaper Contest.

I don't know which, if any of the *Press* staff was there to accept awards that day. I slept in until about 10:30 a.m. in my Carthage apartment, bone weary after a week of teaching at Diamond Middle School.

Ron Graber was kind enough to bring me the results of the contest, as well as the awards I had personally won. After a brief conversation, Ron left. I took the results into my living room and started calculating the Gold Cup Contest for best newspaper in the state. During my time at *The Press*, we had finished fifth four times, always beaten by much larger newspapers.

I was hoping that just one time, since this was my last time, that the newspaper would take fourth place so I could go out a winner.

After I calculated the points, as usual, it was the *Kansas City Star* that won the Gold Cup. The state's second biggest paper, the *St. Louis Post-Dispatch*, took second place...and I rechecked the points at least five times... *The Carthage Press* had finished third! It was the best farewell to the newspaper business I could possibly imagine.

Our series on drunk driving had taken first place in two categories- best investigative reporting and community service. It was the second straight year for us to win the community service award. The previous year we had won it for our Teen Tuesday section. Community service and general excellence were categories in which the MPA awarded extra points to the winners.

Stacy Rector had won first place in the best feature writing category for her Teen Tuesday feature on a high school mother. That same story and Stacy's work on Teen Tuesday enabled The Press to take second place in the best coverage of young people, a category that put us in competition with newspapers of all sizes.

It was Ron's byline that was on the page one article of the November 8, 1999 *Carthage Press* about the MPA awards. I knew immediately, his co-editor, Rick Rogers, had rewritten it.

The headline for the story was "Press captures 14 MPA awards" but my heart sank when I read the subhead- "Press finishes in top 5 ahead of all other southwest Missouri dailies." Rick simply counted the awards. He did not take into consideration our finishes in the categories where extra points were counted. It was the best finish *The Press* had to that point (and remains so 10 years later) and no one would ever know.

*The Press* had won first place for community service and investigative reporting and an 18-year-old reporter had captured first place in the best feature writing category, but that was not what led the coverage:

> *The Carthage Press received five first place awards at this weekend's Missouri Press Association Better Newspaper Contest.*
>
> *Among those honored was Press Editor Rick Rogers, whose Sports Fan section took top honors in the Best Sports Coverage category, and whose contribution to*

*the paper's design earned another first place award.*
*"Creative use of headline style and picture usage," said*
*the judges about the paper's overall appearance. Excellent*
*photos and superb writing vividly display the emotion of*
*sporting events involving local participants and convey*
*the events of importance to the local community," said*
*the judges. "Stories are packaged beautifully and invite*
*interest even from those not from Carthage area. Other*
*sports editors should look at Press's sports photos page and*
*emulate them. Easily the best of the class.*

The article was already five column inches long and there
had been no mention of the community service or investigative
reporting awards. That came in the next paragraph:

*Last year's series by Jo Ellis, Randy Turner, Rogers, John*
*Hacker, and Cait Purinton titled "License to Kill" on drunk*
*driving earned two first place awards, for Best Investigative*
*Reporting and also for Best Community Service. "Excellent*
*job reminding readers how important this subject could be.*
*Personal stories of those affected by drunken driving, and*
*court interpretations bring subject to life. Powerful leads.*
*Really digs down into the meat of a continuing and terrible*
*problem. Good quotes and sources."*

The amount of space for our drunk driving series was less
than half of what was allotted to Rick's sports pages and design.
By this time, it shouldn't have mattered to me. But it did.

The article next turned its attention to Stacy Rector's award:

*Stacy Rector's "Overcoming Obstacles" story on*
*teen mother Jacque Davis took first place in the Best*
*Feature Story category and also helped earn The Press*
*a second place award in Best Young People's Coverage.*
*"Good subject that many families can relate to," said the*
*judges. "Subject isn't touched upon much- the challenges*
*pregnant school girls face. I like that you addressed a*

*teenage mother and praised her accomplishments. Few papers would do this. Also, Teen Tuesday is a neat idea. It encourages young people to read the paper instead of watching television news. The features were excellent. We rarely pause to focus on teens unless something tragic has occurred."*

*Carthage Press* readers probably found this ironic since by the time this article was published, Teen Tuesday had long since been discontinued.

> *Other second place awards went to Rogers for his "Home Away From Home" story and Turner for his "Question of Faith" story.*

It's a shame Rick couldn't have mentioned that the Question of Faith story was also a part of our award-winning drunk driving series. It was the story of the Phipps family of Lamar that was devastated by a 1995 drunk driving accident that killed one family member and permanently damaged two others.

> *Press Editor Ron Graber, Brooke Pyle and Turner took third place in the Best News Story category for their coverage of Carthage native Janet Kavandi's trip into space last summer. "Reporters and photographers went all out to cover a local woman who achieved her dream, and it was a big dream," said the judges. "Writing brings home how excited the town was to see one of its own in space."*

Ron also took a second place in the best news photo category, while Rick finished third in best sports photograph. *The Press* grabbed a fourth place in the Best Advertising Idea-Outside Advertiser category.

I was also disappointed in the use of photos to accompany the story. Mug shots of Rick, Ron, and Jo Ellis were featured. I certainly did not expect to see a photo of John Hacker or me, but pictures of the three young reporters who won awards, Stacy Rector, Cait Purinton, and Brooke Pyle, would have been nice. Especially Stacy, since she was probably the youngest person to ever win a first place plaque in the Missouri Press Association Better Newspaper Contest.

All in all, the article was another signal to me that not only were my days at *The Press* done, but nothing was left of what I had tried to accomplish during my nine and a half years there. Content and substance had been replaced by flash and fluff.

◆     ◆     ◆

Awards are not the reason I went into journalism, but it always gives a reporter a good feeling to be recognized by his or her peers.

During that last turbulent year at *The Carthage Press,* the newspaper won 19 awards, including the 14 at the Missouri Press Association.

Against stiff competition, we were awarded first place in the community service category in the annual Kansas City Press Club Heart of America Awards for our "License to Kill' drunk driving series, beating entries from the *Kansas City Star* and the *Topeka Capital-Journal.*

We also won two of the five first place awards and four awards overall in the annual Associated Press Managing Editors (APME) Contest. The first place awards went to Jo Ellis in the Community Affairs/Public Interest category for "Double Dipping," an investigation into a scandal surrounding the Jasper County collector and to me in the Sports Feature category for "Under Mom's Watch," a Sports Talk column I wrote about Carthage Senior High School volleyball player Tysha Lucas' mother, Peggy, as she watched her daughter play her last high school game.

Rick Rogers finished third in that category for his story "Second chance," while Rick, Nick Parker (a stringer), and I were awarded third place in Spot Sports for our coverage of the Carthage Senior High School Football Homecoming.

Ironically, my Sports Feature winner, "Under Mom's Watch," was one of the stories Rick had attempted to cut the end off because it did not fit into his design.

That had been a major bone of contention between Rick and me. Design was everything to Rick. He was willing to lop off the end of a sports feature just so it would not interfere with the aesthetic beauty of his page. On other occasions, he would jump just one or two paragraphs to another page, which not only served as an inconvenience to readers, but It also wreaked havoc on those who wanted to clip the articles and place them in scrapbooks. I admired his passion for making his pages perfect, but to me, the content was always the most important thing. The design had to serve the content, not the other way around.

◆     ◆     ◆

Because of Rick's ascension to co-editor (and essentially editor-in-charge), I was thrown off the track about why I had lost my job. Since Rick had been scheduled to take the job at Missouri Southern State College and all of a sudden he had my old job, it had to be a palace coup. I naturally started thinking about all of the time Rick had spent with Ralph Bush. He had to have been undermining me, telling Ralph how I was standing in the way of *The Carthage Press* becoming a great newspaper, and subtly, or not so subtly, letting Ralph know what miracles he could accomplish if he were put in charge.

I had far too much time on my hands so I did a lot of that kind of thinking. I was 43 years old and had been replaced by someone who was 24 years old and was undoubtedly working for far less money than I had been making. (That, however, is something that I do not know for sure.) It was a paranoid way of thinking, and I kept fueling those thoughts when I read *The Carthage Press* every day.

I looked at the changes Rick had made (and possibly, Ron, too, but in my way of thinking everything had been done by Rick Rogers) and everything seemed to be the complete antithesis of the way I would have done things.

I noted the new personal column Rick began writing, which each week revealed details of his family life. While I had occasionally written about myself, it was invariably in relation to something that was in the news. To me, Rick's column was Erma Bombeck without the humor.

My paranoia was fueled when Alicia Shepard, a reporter for *American Journalism Review*, contacted me, She had been told about what happened to me. The magazine, which explores issues in journalism, was interested in my story as an example of the way decisions were made in newspaper chains like Liberty Group Publishing.

I told her everything I knew, which seemed a lot at that time but not so much as I look back on it 10 years later. A week later, she called me and told me she had run into a dead end. I said I had been fired for one reason, Ralph Bush said it had been for another.

I had noted that in the reader surveys that we had taken, the last one only a few months earlier, my column had been ranked the most popular feature in the newspaper. Ralph Bush told Ms. Shepard that was because I was the one who tallied the ballots.

"It's your word against his on everything," she said. "I would like to follow up on this, but I'm afraid there's no story."

Still wanting to pin down Ralph about the reason for my departure, I sent him a written request for a service letter, something fired employees are allowed to do under Missouri law.

A few days later, I received a cold, impersonal (not that I had expected anything else) response:

*"According to your employee file you were hired on April 2, 1990, to work in the editorial dept. You were promoted to managing editor on November 22, 1993. From the records in your file, I cannot determine what instructions you were given concerning your job description at the time of your promotion. That was under different ownership of the paper and different management. Your responsibilities as managing editor under the current ownership and management were defined as follows:*

— *Management of the editorial staff*
— *Responsibility for news content and all publications of The Carthage Press within the guidelines provided by management*
— *Personally writing a reasonable amount of material for the paper*

*You were terminated on May 17, 1999, for failure to follow guidelines and objectives regarding content of the paper.*

*I hope that this provides the information that you needed.*

◆    ◆    ◆

Though my part of the American Heritage Festival lawsuit had ended five and a half months earlier, *The Carthage Press* and its owner, Liberty Group Publishing, remained a defendant until November 1999.

The end of the lawsuit did not receive the same kind of treatment as the beginning. It was relegated to the bottom of page one, thanks to the demolition of venerable Hawthorne Elementary School, the same school once attended by murder victim Douglas Ryan Ringler.

Ron Graber wrote the story:

*The lawsuit between American Heritage Festival organizer Terry Reed and local law enforcement officials, civic leaders and media representatives has been dropped.*

*A statement released by the law offices of Daniel Clampett Powell and Cunningham, which represented the county officials, states, "The parties to the suit wish to announce that they have resolved their differences. No one is admitting liability and no money will be paid."*

*The lawsuit was filed shortly after the American Heritage Festival was held at Red Oak II in July of 1998. Newspaper articles in the Kansas City Star and The Carthage Press voiced concerns about the possibility of right-wing extremists and hate groups attending the event. Reed says these fears, along with the suspicions of local law enforcement officials, were unjustified.*

*"This country's law enforcement is reacting in a state of hyper-paranoia," Reed recently told The Carthage Press.*

*Reed says that because of the events at Waco, Texas, and Oklahoma City, police had been on the alert to threats to national security and terrorism.*

*Reed said concerns about a Texas organization called "The New Republic" which had members at a preparedness festival, also led to the overreaction of police in this area. He says misleading information given out by the Southern Poverty Law Center also contributed to the problem.*

*"We do know there was a high level meeting held at the Sheriff's Department between the DEA, FBI, and Missouri Highway Patrol," says Reed. "They expected to snare some terrorists. They really have egg on their faces.*

*"It was a good test case of watching people get stampeded," Reed says. "IF I have any animosity it is toward the (Jasper County) Sheriff's Department. This is how Waco happened."*

Reed said that even though the parties in the lawsuit have been "held harmless," he is still upset about the whole event.

"I've still got a foul taste in my mouth," says Reed. "The average citizen doesn't realize how fragile the separation between law enforcement and their civil rights are. When law enforcement falls back into that face-saving mode, they're even more dangerous.

Reed cites Waco as an example.

"Why did law enforcement react the way they did," he asks. "Why did they kill children?"

Reed says he is not the character he has been made out to be. He says he does not have a huge propensity to sue, and that many of the allegations made against him are untrue, such as the accusation that he once hauled cocaine into the airport at Mena, Ark.

Also unfair is the characterization of the American Heritage Festival attendees as racist conservative wackos, says Reed.

"There were no arrests made here at the three-day event, which shows the quality of the attendees," he says. Reed says most of the people at the festival who looked like criminals were actually undercover police.

The statement issued by the county's lawyers states, "The parties, as part of the resolution of their disputes wish to state that none of them have any knowledge on information that would indicate that any offenses were committed at the festival, or that any hate groups attended the festival. There were no known acts of overt racism at the festival. As far as is known, the festival was attended by law abiding citizens from the area and around the nation."

As a result of the issued statement, Reed's lawsuit against Bill Pierce, Steve Weston, Jerry Neil, Edie Neil,

*Danny Hensley and Mark Elliott will be dismissed. Charges against The Carthage Press had previously been dismissed.*

*After the uproar, Reed's plan to purchase Red Oak II fell through. Reed says that he is moving forward with a similar plan elsewhere.*

*"We are proceeding with a $20 million project in Utah," says Reed. "It could have been in Carthage." Reed says the resort, located in Zion National Park, will feature a lodge, hiking and nature trails.*

What an irritating way to end a 16-month nightmare. It was obvious that lawyers had dictated everything about the way the newspaper covered the conclusion of the American Heritage Festival lawsuit, right down to allowing Terry Reed to have one final, uncontested public forum.

Terry Reed's lawsuit cost me my job, but while he was given full rein to deliver his local law enforcement is out of control message, my name was not mentioned even once.

It was during a conversation with someone who worked closely with Ralph Bush at *The Carthage Press* that I finally learned why I had been fired.

In the back of my mind, I knew it was the Terry Reed lawsuit, but my anger at Rick Rogers had blinded me to that. I was told that it was the lawsuit that ended my time at *The Press,* and that Ralph did not have any choice in the matter. It all stemmed from the return of the service for the libel suit.

Oddly enough, I felt a lot better about the end of my journalism career after that. What a way to go out, unlike Bill and Hillary Clinton, who managed to survive everything that was thrown at them…I truly was the victim of a vast right wing conspiracy, even though I was never the target.

As I was researching this book, I discovered something I had totally overlooked before. Terry Reed dismissed me from the lawsuit on May 17, 1999, the same day Ralph Bush fired me.

# *LOOKING TO*
# *THE FUTURE*

*The Carthage Press* was my past. It was time to look toward the future. I had to find a newspaper that wanted to take a chance on damaged goods. Except for a brief period when I was a substitute teacher in the fall of 1982 and a short stint as director of the Granby summer recreation program that same year, the only real jobs I had ever had were with newspapers. Journalism was my life.

And that was my problem.

I answered an advertisement for a managing editor for an Arkansas newspaper. The ad did not specify which newspaper had the opening.

Right after I returned from mailing my resume, the phone rang. 'This is Ed Simpson at the *Joplin Globe*. I heard about what happened to you, Randy. Are you doing all right?"

I lied and told him I was.

"Why don't you come over here and talk with me? We might be able to work something out."

After 17 years of considering the *Joplin Globe* my enemy, during my time at *The Press* and the *Lamar Democrat*, I might go to work there. Wouldn't that be something? It would even mean I would not have to leave Carthage. There was nothing in the world I hated as much as moving.

We set up a meeting for the next afternoon. It was the first time I had ever been in the *Joplin Globe* office. Edgar Simpson greeted me and took me on a quick tour. Before he asked me any questions, he started telling me how he was going to use me at *the Globe*. I was starting to feel an enormous weight had been lifted from my shoulders. I wasn't even going to be unemployed for a week.

When he took me into his office and closed the doors, he began asking me questions, but none of the questions were about my skills or my philosophy of news or anything that might have been remotely connected to a job on the *Joplin Globe's* editorial staff.

Every question was about *The Carthage Press*. What was its circulation? What were the strengths and weaknesses of the people who remained on the *Press* staff? What would the *Globe* have to do to make further inroads into Carthage? I studiously avoided giving away any secrets about *The Press*. Edgar Simpson was not planning to hire me, I surmised quickly. I was only there so he could pump me for information about a competitor.

That was confirmed as our one-hour interview came to a close. "I'm afraid right now our company has a hiring freeze," Simpson said, "but when they give me the word, I will give you a call."

We shook hands, I left the *Joplin Globe* and I knew I would never set foot in that building again.

I watched over the next few weeks as the *Globe* hired two reporters. I never heard from Edgar Simpson.

A few years later, Simpson left the newspaper business to return to his native Ohio to be chief of staff to the newly elected attorney general Marc Dann. That job lasted less than two years, ending with a sexual harassment scandal surrounding Dann. Simpson was subjected to considerable ridicule for the way he handled the situation.

It couldn't have happened to a nicer guy.

# NEWSPAPER JOB POSSIBILITIES

*The Joplin Globe* had no interest in me, which meant that I probably was going to have to pack up my stuff and leave Carthage. There is almost nothing in the world I hate more than moving, but there was only one newspaper in Carthage and one in Joplin and neither one of those had any interest in me.

Let me backtrack on that for a second.

*The Carthage Press* and Publisher Ralph Bush still had interest in me, but not in helping me in any way. A few days after I filed for unemployment insurance benefits, I was stunned to find that the process had been put on hold because Ralph Bush was challenging my right to receive the benefits. That battle took nearly two months before I won, during which time I spent nearly every cent I had remaining.

I found out quickly that other newspapers did not consider being fired by *The Carthage Press* to be a badge of shame.

I had a telephone interview with the publisher of the *Siloam Springs, Arkansas Herald News*, and was asked to come to the paper to interview for the managing editor position. I did not.

I talked with Jimmie Sexton, the owner of the *Neosho Post*, a weekly that was competing with Liberty Group Publishing's *Neosho Daily News* about a position, but no job was offered, and it did not seem to be a good fit for me.

I received a call from Kate Marymont, the *Springfield News-Leader's* managing editor, about my interest in a reporting position there should one become available. I told her I would be interested, but the opportunity never came.

I also received calls from McDonald County Newspapers, another *Neosho Daily News* competitor, and the Fort Smith, Arkansas newspaper, but I never got back with them. And my former publisher at *The Press*, Jim Farley, talked to me briefly about managing three weekly newspapers in Arkansas, but again, the job did not seem to be a good fit.

Two other newspaper suitors were more promising. Randy Battagler, the publisher of the *Nevada Daily Mail*, a newspaper about 50 miles north of Carthage, called me one night in early June and invited me to lunch. He indicated that he wanted to bring me is as managing editor, "but I already have a managing editor."

I was tempted to ask him why we were having lunch if that was the case, but he continued, telling me a story about a newspaper competition in Nevada that had only recently ended with the *Daily Mail* buying out its upstart competitor and, as part of the deal, also receiving its 23-year-old editor.

"Would you be willing to come and do some reporting for us and size up the situation?" he asked.

"I'm not sure I feel comfortable about that."

"I know it doesn't sound good," he said, "but trust me, this would be a great situation for you and this is a good company to work for."

I told Battagler I would think about it, but I had already made up my mind. There was no way in hell I was going to step into that kind of a situation.

I discovered quickly that when Randy Battagler wants something, he goes after it. Three days after our lunch, he called, "Look, this situation is getting worse," he said. I've got a couple of reporters out and this girl (his editor) is having problems. Do you think you can come up here and help me out?"

In the three days since I had talked to Battagler, I had some time to think, and I knew I had been too picky. If I kept on looking for the perfect working situation, I might never work again. On the other hand, Battagler was not going to get me cheap.

"I'll come up for $12 an hour," I said

I thought that would end the conversation. "You've got it," he answered. As the conversation continued, Battagler indicated that if I came to work full time at the *Daily Mail*, he would pay me more than the $26,000 I had received for the last three years I worked at *The Carthage Press*.

So I began my career with the *Nevada Daily Mail*...or so I thought.

When I arrived at the newspaper office the next day, Battagler had apparently changed his mind about how much I would make if I decided to work at his newspaper. Instead of getting paid somewhere in the neighborhood of $28,000 annually, Battagler talked about $23,000 and I found I had to go through another interview...with the woman I was being brought in to replace. I don't know if that was something Battagler wanted, or if she just wanted to size me up.

From the questions she asked, two things were clear- she was out of her league being the managing editor of a daily newspaper, and she did not want me around.

She put me at a desk and told me she would get me an assignment in a little bit. One hour passed, no assignment. Two hours passed, no assignment. It was 11 a.m. As I was reading the *Kansas City Star*, I saw an education story I thought I could localize. I asked the editor if she minded.

"Do what you want to do," she said, appearing exasperated that I was interrupting whatever it was she was doing.

I called the Nevada school superintendent, interviewed him, got my story, and typed it up, all in about 30 minutes. I walked over to the editor. "The story's done. It's on the computer."

"I'll look at it later," she said, not bothering to look up from the letter she was reading.

I returned to my desk and remembered a Vernon County felony case that was being heard in Barton County on a change of venue. I called Barton County Circuit Clerk Jerry Moyer to see if there had been any developments in the case. A hearing had been held earlier in the week, and within a few moments, I had another story.

By noon, I had three stories.

I did not have any other thoughts for stories for that day. The editor did not talk to me for the rest of the afternoon, though I found the other people at the *Daily Mail* to be warm and friendly.

When I returned for the second day, I wrote two more stories by noon. At about 12:30, the editor spoke to me for the first time since the previous morning. "You will need to come back tonight and cover the fair," she said. The activity she wanted me to cover was at eight o'clock.

"That's going to be tough," I said. "I am driving 100 miles round trip.

"That's your problem," she said.

I told her I would not be able to cover that. She pointed out that I was not getting off on the right foot.

"That won't be a problem," I said, heading for the door. On the way out, I stopped by Battagler's office and told him the arrangement was not going to work out. I thanked him for considering me for the job.

"Be sure to fill out your time card before you leave," he said.

My 12 hours at the *Nevada Daily Mail* were over. The newspaper ran all five stories I wrote…and 10 years later, I am still waiting for my $144.

◆          ◆          ◆

After my 12-hour stint at the *Nevada Daily Mail*, I had another thought. Even though 18 years had passed since I had done my student teaching at Diamond Junior High School, I wondered if it was too late to start a career in education.

I had been reading about how desperate some schools were to find teachers and if they were that desperate, heck, one of them might even hire me.

So I applied for two teaching positions that were close to Carthage, a junior high social studies position in the Webb City R-7 School District and a high school social studies job at Diamond.

My resume was geared toward journalism jobs, not teaching positions. Thirty awards for investigative reporting and more than 70 awards overall looked good if you were trying to get hired as a reporter or as an editor. It didn't do me a bit of good if I wanted to teach history to Webb City seventh graders.

I emphasized the internship programs I had for high school and college students when I was at the *Democrat* and *The Press*, and references from some well-respected educators and somehow, I managed to land an interview for the Webb City job.

I had known the Webb City superintendent, Dr. Ron Lankford, for quite some time. Not only had I worked with him on various stories while at *The Press*, but he had also done his student teaching at East Newton High School when I attended there in the early '70s, and my younger sister was one of his students when he later taught at East Newton.

I quickly found out how out of my element I was. The icebreaking part of the interview went well, but once Dr. Lankford began questioning me about how I would handle classroom situations, I was lost. Except for the brief time when I had been a substitute teacher, I had not been in a classroom since May 1981. Times had changed and I could barely remember what I had learned about teaching. I knew I had blown the interview when Dr. Lankford asked about how I would handle classroom discipline. My solution was to keep the class engaged so there would be no discipline problems, which quickly tipped him off that I did not have the slightest idea of how to control an unruly class.

Even though I knew I had little or no chance to getting the job, I was grateful to Dr. Lankford for giving me the interview. It gave me an idea of what I was going to have to learn to get a teaching job. And that was what I really wanted. I     was surprised by how much I wanted to work with kids again.

My favorite part of working at newspapers for the past 14 years had been working with the young reporters and watching their successes. Of course, they were handpicked and if I somehow managed to land a teaching job, I would not have that luxury.

Still, it was tough knowing that I had blown a chance to teach in the best paying school district in southwest Missouri, but it was not long before I was called in to interview for the Diamond job.

Unfortunately, that interview did not go much better than the first one. I was also familiar with this superintendent. Dr. Greg Smith had been an assistant superintendent in the Webb City School District and had been superintendent at Sarcoxie. I had interviewed him just three months earlier when he had been hired at Diamond.

At least when I left the Webb City interview, I thought there was a slim chance I would be hired. When the interview ended at Diamond, I was beginning to wonder if my plan to teach was just a foolish dream.

As I reviewed the interview play-by-play in my mind, I could not think of one thing I had said that might have impressed Dr. Smith.

After failing to get the Diamond job, my next interview was for an alternative school teaching position at my alma mater, East Newton. The school placed at-risk students in a building about a mile from the high school that used to house the Brown Derby Restaurant, an eating establishment where I spent a great deal of time while I was in high school.

That interview went worse than the others.

I had an opportunity to interview for a Gifted K-12 job in the McDonald County School District, but when I found out I would be going to as many as four schools, miles apart, every day, I canceled the interview.

I barely missed out on another teaching job. I mailed in a resume for a high school social studies position at El Dorado Springs. The superintendent, Greg Koetting, whom I had worked with when he held the same position at Jasper, called and told me the position had already been filled, but he added that had he known I was looking for a teaching job the position would have been mine.

That did not make me feel any better.

◆          ◆          ◆

At about the time I was interviewing at Diamond and Webb City, I received an e-mail from Floyd Jernigan, the publisher of the *Miami, Oklahoma News-Record*. He asked if I would be interested in evaluating his newspaper. I agreed to do so and a couple of days later, a week's worth of *News-Records* arrived in the mail.

I was not impressed with the newspaper. The writing was poor, the photos only a little better, and the papers were almost the same every day, boring government coverage, almost no features or lively local columns, and a sports section that leaned far too heavily on Associated Press.

Still, I did not want to hurt Jernigan's feelings, so when I e-mailed my evaluation, I emphasized the few good things I saw- the fact that page one was almost entirely local, something that is absolutely necessary in a day and age when national and international news is readily available elsewhere and on a more timely basis. I noted one government article that had more than the usual amount of digging, though not by much.

It did not take long for Jernigan to return my e-mail. He was far from satisfied with my evaluation. "I am not wanting to read good things about my newspaper," he wrote. "Don't pull any punches."

After that, I took my time going through each edition and when I sent the second e-mail, I did not have many good things to say about the *Miami News-Record*.

The next day, Jernigan called me and revealed why he wanted me to evaluate his newspaper. "Our managing editor is leaving. I like the things you said about the *News-Record*. It sounds like we share some of the same views on how a newsroom should be run. Would you be interested in interviewing for the job?"

I had almost completely convinced myself that my future was in teaching. I was even considering being a full-time substitute teacher just to get my foot in the door, but this would be a regular paid position. And though I had my heart set on teaching, I still loved being a reporter and being around a newspaper. If Floyd Jernigan wanted me to be managing editor of the *Miami News-Record*, all he had to do was guarantee me two things, I decided. I wanted the same freedom to be a reporter/editor that I had at *The Carthage Press*, and I wanted $30,000 a year.

But Jernigan was not about to turn over the newspaper that easily. First, I had to go through an informal telephone interview with him.

After that, another publisher in the Boone Newspapers chain that owned the *News-Record* interviewed me. Boone Newspapers at one time had owned the *Lamar Democrat*. The publisher, from the Fergus Falls, Minnesota, newspaper interviewed me for more than an hour.

Apparently, the Minnesota publisher and Jernigan liked what they heard. Jernigan scheduled me for an 11:30 a.m. interview the following Tuesday.

I left Carthage early Tuesday morning, wanting to make sure I arrived in Miami early. As I was driving through Webb City, I noticed a car pulling out from a side road about a quarter of a mile ahead of me; several other cars had pulled up to the stop sign. As I continued, in the rear view mirror I noticed a police car coming up from behind me. Ever since my investigation into the Webb City Police Department from 1990 to 1992, I had made sure to be especially careful as I drove through the city. I checked my speedometer and I was going well under the speed limit. I had been driving straight through with no turns, so there could not possibly be any turn signal violations. I figured the policeman was probably just going my way, and then the red light and the siren came on.

I pulled over and waited as the policeman exited his cruiser and walked up to my door. "State law says you have to pull over for a funeral procession," he said, after he examined my license.

"I didn't realize it was a funeral procession."  I told him I was headed for a job interview. "I guess I had my mind on the interview."

After he checked my license with the dispatcher, he let me off with a warning and I left Webb City driving about 15 miles under the speed limit.

When I arrived at the *News-Record*, I was ushered into Jernigan's office. He went over my critique of his newspaper and asked some follow-up questions. After that, he asked questions about how I would handle coverage of certain community events.

When noon arrived, he buzzed in his advertising and circulation managers, and moments later, we were headed for one of Miami's best restaurants.

I liked the way this was going. These guys were pulling out all of the stops for me. After lunch, the discussion continued. It was apparent that Jernigan was going to offer me the job.

He readily agreed that I would be a reporter/editor and not a page-pusher.

"Randy, we are aware of what you bring to a newspaper. We don't want to change any of that. I talked to Ralph Bush about you."

Uh-oh.

"He said you were a top-notch editor and reporter."

Then why did he fire me?     I did not verbalize that thought.

"We want you here. We want you to turn the *News-Record* into the best small town newspaper in Oklahoma." At that moment, Jernigan's secretary entered with two sheets of paper in her hand and handed them to the publisher.

"This is what we are willing to offer you," Jernigan said and handed me the papers. I noticed the traditional two weeks of vacation after one year, health insurance, and mileage reimbursement that was more than *The Press* had paid. At the bottom of the first sheet, I saw what my salary would be-$29,800 a year.

It was $200 below my $30,000 requirement. It had to be a sign. At the same time, I kept thinking, "This is $3,800 a year more than I made at *The Press*. This is more money than I have ever made anywhere in my entire life."

I carefully examined the papers. "Is this $29,800 set in stone?" I asked.

Jernigan said, it was, but he added, "If you reach the goals we set for you, you can make another $2,000 in bonus money."

$31,800. That was over $30,000, but it was not guaranteed. I realized I did not want to make an immediate decision about the offer.

"Can I have until the end of the week to think about this?" I asked, explaining that I was still considering taking a teaching position (though none had been offered to me).

Jernigan agreed and told me he would call me back at about noon on Friday.

I had three days to make the most important decision of my 43 years- was I going to make more money than I had ever made in my life and do what I had been doing for 22 years or was I going to substitute teach for about $60 or $70 a day, with no guarantee of whether I would work from one day to the next?

When I returned to Carthage, I checked the education jobs posted at the Missouri Southern State College and Southwest Missouri State University (now Missouri State University) websites. Nothing was available. It was already the end of July. It was highly doubtful that any openings would pop up in the couple of weeks before Missouri schools were back in session.

I checked again on Wednesday and found no new job openings. I checked on an April listing for a high school social studies position, but it had been filled months earlier.

On Thursday, I visited my parents in Newtonia. While there, I had a sudden urge to check once again for job openings. There were no new ones on the Missouri Southern website. I almost called it quits there, but I decided to check out SMSU.

And there it was.

"Writing teacher wanted- Diamond Middle School. Contact Ron Mitchell, middle school principal, or Robert Blizzard, high school principal." I jotted down the number, ran to the phone…and immediately dialed a wrong number.

I rechecked the number and dialed again. This time, I heard a voice answer, "Diamond Schools." I asked for Ron Mitchell. I had known Ron for more than a decade since the time he attended Liberal High School and I covered some of his football and basketball games for the *Lamar Democrat*. I did not count on that helping me much since knowing Ron Lankford had not landed me a job at Webb City, and knowing

Greg Smith had not helped me in my earlier attempt to be hired for a teaching job at Diamond.

"Mr. Mitchell is not here at the moment."

I asked for Robert Blizzard.

"Mr. Blizzard is not here at the moment," the woman said.

I explained why I was calling and asked, "Is there anyone there I can talk to?"

"Dr. Smith is in," she said.

"Could I talk to him?"

Seconds later, he was on the phone. "Dr. Smith, this is Randy Turner, I just saw your advertisement for a writing teacher. This one is right up my alley and I would love to interview for it."

I did not like the way that sounded coming from my mouth, but it did not seem to bother Dr. Smith. "Randy, Ron Mitchell will be back later this afternoon. I will have him give you a call."

Ron Mitchell's call came five minutes later and we set up a 9:30 a.m. interview for the next day. If I were lucky, I would have a teaching job by the time Floyd Jernigan called to find out if he had a new managing editor.

For some reason, the interview, which was with both Ron Mitchell and Greg Smith, went much smoother than my previous Diamond interview. After 20 minutes, Ron told me he had two more applicants to interview and he would let me know by five o'clock.

After I thanked him and left the superintendent's office, I realized it was time for me to make my decision. Jernigan was going to call at noon, five hours before I would know if I had the Diamond position.

I continued to think about it after I returned to my apartment. At 11:45, Floyd Jernigan called. "Do we have a new managing editor, Randy?"

I did not know what I was going to say until I heard the words coming out of my mouth. "Floyd, I appreciate the offer, but I have a teaching job. I'm afraid I'm going to have to turn you down."

He wished me luck.

Two minutes after our conversation ended, Ron Mitchell called. "Congratulations. We are offering you a contract."

And with those words, I left journalism and became a teacher. I turned down $29,800 a year (and a possible $2,000 in bonus money), and signed a contract for $21,450 a year.

And I couldn't remember ever being happier.

# SCHOOL DAYS

I was the final teacher hired by the Diamond R-4 School District for the 1999-2000 school year. The class I would teach, called creative language arts, was essentially a writing class, I was told by Principal Ron Mitchell as I reported to work the following Monday after I was hired.

I would be teaching a seventh grade class, two eighth grade classes, a sixth grade class, and two classes with both seventh and eighth graders.

Then he took me to my classroom. I had wondered if I might by some stroke of luck be put in the same classroom in which I did my student teaching 18 years earlier, but that was not to be the case.

I did not say a word as we left the principal's office, which was in a small building outside of the school and headed toward a trailer located by the high school gymnasium.

As we entered the trailer, I did not spend any time thinking about how different it was from the classrooms I had spent time in during my student teaching, substitute teaching, and journalism days. It didn't matter. This was my classroom.

And I had no idea what to do with it.

Ron left me to get used to my new work area and I walked around it, getting the feel of what I hoped would be the change I needed in my life.

I was so engrossed in what I was doing that I did not hear someone coming up the steps. "Hi" a female voice called out and I turned around to see a small, dark-haired girl, whom I took to be one of my students.

"What happened to Mr. Tash?" the girl said referring to my predecessor. I told her Darrel Tash had been moved to a teaching position in the high school.

"I'm Mister Turner," I said. It was the first time I had used the name. I liked it. And the girl, a sixth grader named Maggie Bowman, was the first student I met, and would be in my first hour class on the first day of school later that week. I talked with her a while until her brother, T. J. who would be one of my eighth grade students that first year, and their mother arrived.

A couple of days later when the first faculty meetings was held, I discovered just how comfortable things were going to be. Not only did I know Dr. Smith and Ron Mitchell, but the faculty members were also familiar to me. I remembered Larry Augustine, Larry Doenning, Dotty Doenning, and Nancy Berry from my student teaching days. I remembered Larry Cunningham (they loved to hire people named Larry at Diamond) from my days of covering area sports.

The social studies teacher, Grant Reed, I knew from his days as a teacher and head football coach at Jasper High School. One of the sixth grade language arts teachers, Karen Loewe, had been an assistant high school volleyball and girls basketball coach at Carthage.

One of the elementary teachers, Merri Brummett, had actually been one of my students when I was student teaching, as was Brenda Bradley, one of the secretaries.

The only bad thing I discovered from my first faculty meeting was my standing in the Diamond Middle School Language Arts Department.

Not only was I the only first year teacher among the three of us, but both Karen Loewe and Renee Houk, stood six feet tall, while I was just a shade under five feet nine.

The teachers and staff went out of their way to make me feel comfortable.

The next day, for the first time, I stood in front of a class of my own. This was not a group of kids I was babysitting as a substitute teacher or taking for a few weeks as a student teacher, this was my class.

This was where I wanted to be.

◆          ◆          ◆

As the weeks went on, I found that for the first time I was becoming a morning person. It really does make a difference to be heading home sometime between 4 p.m. and 6 p.m. instead of working until well past midnight.

I also had more energy than I had during my last few years at *The Carthage Press.*

A few weeks after my teaching career began, I was buying groceries at the Wal-Mart Supercenter in Carthage, when I ran into two of my fellow co-defendants from the Terry Reed lawsuit, Jasper County Chief Deputy Jerry Neil and his wife, county recorder Edie Swingle Neil.

After some small talk, Edie said, "Randy, you really are looking much better these days. Teaching has been good for you."

It was not the first time I had heard that comment, nor would it be the last. And I responded the same way each time.

"Why didn't you tell me I looked that bad? I would have become a teacher a long time ago."

It was a funny line, but it was not true. I love teaching and cannot imagine doing anything else, but I would not trade my 22 years as a reporter for anything.

I had a chance to learn from talented co-workers, meet hundreds of fascinating people, and make friends who have stood by me over the years.

I had a great time. It was a heck of a ride.